Herding Cats and Other Alien Creatures

Also by Southern Indiana Writers' Group

The Indian Creek Anthology Series:

Indian Creek Anthology

Ghost Writers

Christmas Bizarre

Dragon: Our Tales

Grounds for Suspicion

2000 Tales

Way Out West

Unbridled Lust

There's Something Under the Bedtime Stories

Novel Ingredients

Write of Passage

Off the Rack

Beastly Tales

It's Always Something

Most Wanted

Future Perfect: Tense in Space

Holiday Bizarre

Pair of Normal What?

The Worst Book in the Universe

XX: SIW Goes Platinum

Also by SIW:

Ghosts: On the Square ... And Elsewhere

Visit the Authors at:

southernindianawriters.com

Herding Cats
and Other
Alien Creatures

Southern Indiana
Writers' Group

Per Bastet

Herding Cats and Other Alien Creatures
The Indian Creek Anthology Series, Volume 21

Published by Per Bastet Publications LLC, P.O. Box 3023 Corydon, IN 47112

Cover art by T. Lee Harris
Spacesuit Photo: NASA

ISBN 978-1-942166-34-4

Herding Cats
and Other
Alien Creatures

Table of Contents

Foreword

As I was reading, in the recent English translation of Alice Herdan-Zuckmayer's *The Farm in the Green Mountains*, the chapter called "Confusion in the Chicken Yard," I reflected on the theme of this twenty-first volume of the Indian Creek Anthology Series. Herdan-Zuckmayer's book is a memoir about the author and her husband Carl's experience, as political refugees from Nazi Germany during the first half of the Forties, running a farm in backwoods Vermont. Neither she nor Zuck, as Alice called him, were experienced farmers. So the account of their time in that American wilderness – with its echoes of some of the more remote rural communities in southern Indiana – was full of humorous adventures as they labored to herd those chickens and other farm animals into some semblance of order.

The "herdee" in question, in this passage, was Hermann, an ungovernable goose who was enamored of a duck and violently resisted their being housed every night in separate sections of the poultry shed. "Without the broom," Herdan-Zuckmayer writes, "we could not have controlled Hermann, who was wild and dangerous. In fact, the broom often played an important role in driving the animals home, in separating fighters, and in self-defense."

All the farm animals, except for the goats who liked "to nibble at the broom straw," were afraid of it. All they had to do was "hold the broom in front of [them], like a witch who is ready to mount her broomstick to ride to the Blocksberg, and the animals scattered and took flight in the desired direction.

"Even the hair on the cats began to stand on end, and they arched their backs and started to spit when the stubby face of the broom approached them. It seemed almost like a magical fear of the witchly attributes that made the animals run away."

A sort of writerly magic exists in the collaborative effort that has brought together these nine stories, two poems, and single work of creative nonfiction in this latest production of the Southern Indiana Writers' Group. In "Herding Cats," the poem that opens the volume, Jen Selinsky speaks of the magician's act involved in bringing together such a "wild assortment" of writers and authorial visions, both in person and in these pages. She is followed in almost seamless transition by Marian Allen's fast-paced, antic, police comedy-drama "By the Book," which places the literary arts where they belong at the center of sentient life: the action unfolds on the planet Llannonn, in and around a "Living Library" ("a group home for people who chose to make careers out of memorizing stories and novels and reciting themselves to anyone of good character who presented a library card") where quick-drawing and impassioned Assistant Librarian Holly Jahangiri leads the charge against a band of ruffians who have been waylaying some of the Living Books.

From across the pond in Great Britain, our own "alien" writer, Andrea Gilbey, contributes "A Furry at the Bottom of My Garden, or, The Cat Who Fell to Earth." What, on the surface, is a charming comedy of errors, in Andrea's deft hands becomes also a comprehending glimpse into the lonely experience of "otherness." She does this with a lightness of touch capable of planting, in the garden at the bottom of her readers' hearts, a resurgence of compassion in this world of competing nationalisms that are so quick to place human beings in boxes or shipping containers stamped with such dehumanizing labels as "illegal" or "alien" or "refugee."

The two pieces that follow, J. Baumgartle's fictional "Cat Power" and Janet Wolanin Alexander's memoiristic "Humans: Herders or Herdees?" share the anthropomorphic conceit of being narrated by the little furries at stories' center: in Baumgartle's story, which shares some of the social consciousness hidden at the heart of Andrea's tale, the narrating cat is instrumental in preventing a minor environmental atrocity; in Alexander's, the series of cats who have insinuated themselves into the lives of "the Js" (Jim and Jan) make the case for a re-ordering of that structure of influence.

"Leader of the Pack" is Brenda Drexler's whimsical recasting of the Shangri-Las' 1965 hit, its feline dialogue connecting it happily with Disney's anti-tragedy *The Aristocats*. Ginny Fleming's hilarious "Cat-A-Strophic Spelling," for its part, makes lemonade out of an almost-tragic metamorphosis that, through some seriously bad "spelling" (of the magical, not orthographic sort), takes an apparently mismatched pair of human lovers in a direction in part feline, but ultimately and rather sweetly canine.

The "wistful lion" that, in Baumgartle's elegant poem, "hauls itself slowly upright from the pride-scented grass" to survey its landscape, would seem to beckon toward the guardian goyle and its kitten-goyles in the richly imagined fantasy world of Bonnie Abraham's "Out of the Cabinet." Mistress Playit Wrenmother and her "small covey of future mages" paint a subtly humorous picture as they traipse through the school of wizardry and surrounding city, engaged in some of their own at-once less catastrophic and more cosmically significant spelling than the lemons-to-lemonade spelling of Fleming's story.

Abraham's fantasy, with its almost Biblical overtones, leads to the Lakota Sioux spirituality underlying the science fiction of T. Lee Harris's "Ghost in the Machine," in which Captain Miranda Morningstar, a United Americas Marine Corps Ghost Walker, is called on to investigate an explosion that shook the asteroid where they are based; only, in a process that her shaman called "the snapping of the tether between body and spirit," her spirit leaves the body behind in anticipation of her mission. T. Lee's story is full of darkness, light, and the vicarious thrill of mortal combat with some truly nefarious alien creatures.

Returning, at last, in "Covenant Restored," to the familiar mortality of this present Earth, Glenda Mills explores the making and sundering of human relationships from a Catholic perspective; her narrative is one woman's inner struggle that lands, with hope but no more assurance than any of life's ventures, in a new romantic attachment whose initial promise is to be sealed with the purchase of a cat. And finally, I offer my own somewhat dark-edged (but ultimately exultant) romantic comedy, "Courting Mel," whose struggling middle-aged lovers – heads of a colorfully eccentric Mormon family – find their way, before a backdrop of looming war in Iraq and a rebellious teenage daughter's dalliance with a biker several years her senior, through their own crisis of faith and love.

I am much indebted, in this my first year editing SIW's Indian Creek anthology, to Marian Allen and T. Lee Harris with their twenty years of previous experience; but also to the club's other members, old and new, in particular those who have lent me their excellent writing. It is without the slightest hesitation that I recommend our combined labor to a reading public that completes our sister- and brotherhood of lovers of the incomparable magic of good writing. We hope that you will be at once entertained and edified by our work.

Brett Alan Sanders
September 2017

Herding Cats

Jen Selinsky

Gathering such a
Wild assortment is
Far from easy,
Especially when one
Considers all the
Hurdles of daily life.

Though times have been
Established, other
Elements often go
Against the clock.
Whether by force
Or choice, it does
Not really matter;
Our absences always
Leave a void.

Getting certain parties
Together is like
Herding cats, I'm often told,
And we are our own clowder.

Those outside looking in,
Though not ignorant
Of our plight,
Could never know all
The complexities involved
In trying to come together.

❋

Only when others realize
The importance of our
Gatherings will they see
The light in knowing what
We are trying to do – write!

By the Book
Marian Allen

Patrolman Pel Darzin, of the Meadow of Flowers district in Council City on the planet Llannonn, waited for Parlormaid Tambar Miznalia to take his card upstairs. He loved libraries, but he'd never been in this kind before. This was a Living Library: a group home for people who chose to make careers out of memorizing stories and novels and reciting themselves to anyone of good character who presented a library card.

The Living Books of this particular library were classics of Terra – or, as the citizens of that planet chose to call themselves, Earth.

This part of the building was, he now read in the news item that scrolled up a wall screen, furnished in the manner of an Anglo Terran boarding house of 1901. The intricately patterned carpet, the unidentifiable knick-knacks cluttering every flat surface, and the superior sniff of the parlormaid who had grudgingly admitted him to the living quarters made him want to go back outside and wipe his boots again.

Stiff upper back, he chided himself, tucking his helmet under his arm and heel-clicking to attention. This had to be done, even if it cost him his beloved job.

*

"Another one of our Books is missing," Assistant Librarian Holly Jahangiri said to her superior. "Three Men in a Boat (To Say Nothing of the Dog) should have been back yesterday, and the patron has vid of him leaving the house and turning toward home."

"Afoot?" Head Librarian Devra Langsam looked up from her monitor, fingertips twitching with the data flow Holly had interrupted.

Holly nodded. "Should I call the constabulary?"

"What did they say the last time we called them?"

"That Books go astray sometimes. One of them quoted a Terran proverb to me: 'Leave them alone and they'll come home wagging their tales behind them.' He *said* it was a Terran proverb, anyway. *I* never heard it."

"Nor I." Head Librarian Devra Langsam lowered her fidgety fingertips to the desk on either side of her keypad and let them tap as she thought. "Right," she said at last. "We handle it ourselves."

"I was hoping you'd say that." Holly leaned toward the computer's audio pick-up on her boss' desk. "Computer. Databases. Assistant Librarian Holly Jahangiri. Living Book attrition."

A spreadsheet appeared on the screen.

"Computer, sort by date."

Columns sorted themselves.

Head Librarian Devra Langsam whistled in the universal sign for *That was so cool.*

Assistant Librarian Holly Jahangiri ran a finger down the date column and said, "The attrition is accelerating."

"But we haven't –"

Holly held up a *Wait for it* finger and said, "Computer, sort by date first, then location."

The columns realigned, and this time Devra's whistle meant, *Holy macanoli, would you look at that!*

"We lost one. Then two and then these three, not from us but also here in Capital City, then –" Holly touched the screen and it split into two displays, one the spreadsheet and one empty. "Computer, second screen, map of attrition, animate."

A map of the city came up. A green light appeared at their address. Then more lights, and more, and the city map became an area map, and a district map.

"I see," said Head Librarian Devra Langsam. "Whatever it is that's happening is spreading."

A knock at the door interrupted.

"Come in."

Parlormaid Tambar Miznalia entered and handed Head Librarian Devra Langsam a calling card.

"A constable," Parlormaid Tambar Miznalia said. "Quite low-ranking. His feet are so flat, he'd hydroplane on damp pavement."

"A constable! Excellent! Low-ranking or not, at least the constabulary take us seriously, after all. Send him up. And bring tea. Earl Grey. Hot."

Parlormaid Tambar Miznalia sniffed in a superior way, but nodded.

"And cake," Assistant Librarian Holly Jahangiri added. "Fresh."

*

Patrolman Pel Darzin hooked thumbs with each woman, stumbling over Assistant Librarian Holly Jahangiri's name.

She repeated it for him. "It's spelled H-o-l-l-y. It's a Terran name."

"I like it," he assured her. "Very pretty. Exotic."

Head Librarian Devra Langsam cleared her throat. "Thank you for coming, Patrolman Pel Darzin. I am most concerned about these disappearances."

"So am I."

Devra, as head librarian, took on the role of spokesperson for the library. "You? As in you as a constable or you, personally?"

The patrolman fidgeted with his helmet.

Parlormaid Tambar Miznalia entered, carrying a tray of tea and cake. Patrolman Pel Darzin moved as if to take it from her, but she sniffed at him and he stepped back. She put the tray on a table in the corner.

"Will there be anything else, M'm?"

"No, thank you," said Head Librarian Devra Langsam. "But get a handkerchief, will you? That sniffing is getting on my nerves."

Head Librarian Devra Langsam invited Patrolman Pel Darzin to sit and rest his helmet. Assistant Librarian Holly Jahangiri passed around the tea and cake.

"Speak to me," Devra urged him, when he had washed a bite of cake down with a gulp of sweet milky tea.

"I have this friend," he said. "A Living Book. Retired. From the Living Library at Overturf."

"Retired?" Devra raised her left eyebrow, a capability of which she was inordinately proud. "Most of our Books retire *to* it, not *from* it."

"So he tells me. But he lost a couple of good friends: The Life and Death (But Mostly the Death) of Erica Flynn and Catcher in the Rye. So my friend retired and went undercover."

Holly bit her lips but couldn't help herself. "If he's undercover, how do you get hold of him? Page him?"

Pel Darzin regarded her reproachfully and said, "I phone him."

"Well, then," said Head Librarian Devra Langsam, "phone him."

*

Kurt Maxxon hooked thumbs with the librarians and greeted Pel Darzin with a friendly nod. He introduced himself as Kurt Maxxon–just plain Kurt Maxxon.

Head Librarian Devra Langsam did her left eyebrow trick. "No title?"

"Not while I'm undercover. When this case is solved, I'll take my titles back. All of them."

"All of them?"

Constable Pel Darzin beamed with commendable pride in his friend. "Kurt was the Kurt Maxxon *series*. Kurt Maxxon, detective."

Holly gasped. "I love those! We have some of those, ourselves! Individual titles, though. We've never had a Boxed Set."

Devra was impressed, in spite of her obligation, as a librarian, to play it cool.

"The constable seems to think you can help us with our problem, Retired Living Book Kurt Maxxon."

"I hope I can. These aren't just texts, you know; they're people."

"We are aware of that," Devra said, with genuine coldness. "One doesn't spend twenty years of one's life as housemother to a Living Library without knowing the humanity of your charges. Especially when they decide to have a pillow fight after lights-out."

"Or a food fight," Holly added.

"Or a food fight," Devra echoed, with feeling. "Why don't you sit down and help yourself to tea and cake. Then you can tell us what you know, and we'll show you what we –" A totally accidental joggle of her elbow on the part of her assistant caused her to spill her tea and correct herself. "We'll show you what Assistant Librarian Holly Jahangiri has discovered."

"It's like this," Maxxon said. "When my pals didn't return themselves after two weeks, the librarian phoned the client. She said she read both of them in the first week and sent them back. Naturally, the librarian didn't take her word for it, but truth serum verified her story."

Assistant Librarian Holly Jahangiri pulled up her spreadsheet and map using the new touch-screen technology that was replacing the vocal commands that could cause so much chaos in an office with loudmouths in nearby cubicles.

"Right here. Not among the first disappearances, but fairly early. Overturf isn't far from Capital City."

She showed Maxxon how the problem had spread.

He nodded. "Whatever it is, it started in Capital City. And if you look at your figures carefully, you'll see that the increase in disappearances is due to the spreading. Fewer Books are disappearing from any one place."

"We lost two just the other day. The Eloquent Scribe and Sideshow in the Center Ring. One has a male narrator and one a female, but she's old enough to be his grandmother, so don't try to tell me they've probably run off together." Holly gave Darzin a stink-eye so stinky that, even though "probably ran off together" *would* have been the official response, he affected a look of shocked denial.

"*Be that as it may*," said Maxxon, "it looks like a fad. Starts in the capital and spreads to the sticks."

"But they don't have libraries in the provinces," Devra said.

"Don't they?" Maxxon looked straight at Holly, who flushed, then paled.

"You really *are* a detective series, aren't you? How could you tell?"

"That purple feather boa in the outer office was my first clue. It was the only outer garment there; chances were it belonged to the Assistant Librarian, not the Head Librarian. When I got in here, I saw Head Librarian Devra Langsam's houndstooth cape on her peg, so I knew I was right. When I met you, I noted your firm thumb-hook. Finally, I spotted the spikeflower behind your ear. Nobody wears a spikeflower except rurals from Meadow of Flowers Province on Spikeflower Festival Day."

Constable Darzin and the librarians applauded enthusiastically.

"You didn't answer the question," Devra said, as the accolade faded. "Do they have libraries in the provinces or don't they?"

"Not ... ordinary libraries."

Devra raised her other eyebrow, just to prove she could. "Clarify."

"We call them storytellers. They ... tell stories. Like Books, only they've never been written down. Each one is a unique collection of stories. They wander the countryside, going from house to house and village to village, stopping wherever they're given shelter."

"So," Maxxon said, "if one went missing, how would anyone know?"

"Eventually, people would say, 'I haven't heard old Stories To Scare The Pee Out Of You lately, have you?' or, 'I'd like to treat my girl to a romantic evening listening to Fiery Heroes of Desire Who Look Just Like Your Boyfriend,' but nobody knows where he is.' I don't know if or when anybody would realize a storyteller had disappeared."

"We would know," Darzin said. "Storytellers are licensed yearly."

Neither of the librarians had known that.

"All the storytellers are accounted for. I checked before I came here today."

"So," Holly said, "whatever is happening is only happening to what we might call formal texts."

"Or," said Maxxon, "foreign ones. The storytellers' collections are native to our planet, aren't they?"

"Naturally," said Holly. "A lot of them date from before off-worlders started coming here." She leaned closer to the pick-up on Devra's desk. "Computer, sort missing Books by planet of origin."

Devra gave a sharp nod when she saw the result. "Terran, every one of them."

"Translated," Darzin asked, "or in the original Terran languages?"

Holly gave the sort order. "The original Terran language. *Language*, singular. All in English."

"Terran expatriots?" Pel Darzin hoped not. He hadn't yet had to deal with aliens from outer space, and wasn't sure he ever wanted to.

Kurt Maxxon stood and paced. "Is there any pattern to the disappearances? I suppose if they had all vanished on their way to or from the same place, that would show in your records."

Devra called up a program and scanned it. "No such pattern."

A brouhaha downstairs penetrated the padded sanctum of the Head Librarian. It grew to a hubub as it clattered up the stairs. Assistant Librarian Holly Jahangiri hustled to the outer office to intercept it before it could disturb her boss. As Kurt Maxxon, Pel Darzin, and, in spite of her librarianesque imperturbability, Devra Langsam crowded out to see what was happening, she needn't have bothered.

The door to the outer office swung open and Parlormaid Tambar Miznalia rushed in, eyes wide, all pose of superiority gone.

"Oh, Head Librarian! Oh, Assistant Head Librarian! He's back, but they've hurt him! He barely escaped with his life!"

"Who?" The four sleuths, had Tambar Miznalia ever heard of owls, would have reminded her of a tree full of them.

"Three Men in a Boat!"

Holly was quick to notice the parlormaid's omission of the subtitle. Was there more here than the natural distress of a library employee at the misuse of a volume?

Head Librarian Devra Langsam took charge, fixing the beaded hairclip which was her badge of office more firmly in her hair. "Where is he?"

"In Repairs." Parlormaid Tambar Miznalia sniffed, then blew her nose heartily into a white handkerchief the size of a tablecloth. In fact, it was a tablecloth; Darzin recognized it from one of the occasional tables in the entrance hall.

*

Repairs, in a Living Library, was a combination infirmary, costumery, and media center. It was where Books went if they were ill or injured (up until now, always by accident), when they needed their period native Terran costumes altered, mended or replaced, and to refresh their memories on their texts.

Devra explained this to Maxxon and Darzin, while Holly provided what comfort she could to the distraught parlormaid by the traditional Llannonninn method of patting her on the shoulder and murmuring, "There, there."

The physician/costumer/media specialist was a tall, slim, competent genius with a blue mohawk. She went by the professional name Saradeeh. No one knew what her birth name was. She was mysterious without being creepy.

The Book sitting on the exam table before her was a young man of dark coloring and a somewhat vacant look.

Parlormaid Tambar Miznalia sobbed when she saw him and pattered across the room to leap onto the table and into his arms.

"Damage report," said the head librarian. "I'm speaking to you, Repairperson Saradeeh, since Three Men in a Boat (To Say Nothing of the Dog) appears to be occupied."

Tambar Miznalia tore herself away only long enough to turn her head and sniff. And she meant it to sting.

Repairperson Saradeeh huffed and tossed her sewing kit aside.

"Nothing serious. He's been in a bit of a scuffle. Lost a button, which I was going to sew back on, but it appears I'll have to do an emergency parlormaidectomy before that happens. Also seems to have lost his hat, a straw boater with a red hatband, imported regardless of cost from the Susquehanna Hat Company."

"Chap knocked it off," said Three Men in a Boat (To Say Nothing of the Dog).

"Oh," said Head Librarian Devra Langsam, with the industrial-strength sarcasm available only by prescription for librarians, "did you notice there are other people in the room?"

"I say," said the young man.

One doesn't become Head Librarian by missing one's chances. Before his attention could be reclaimed by his beloved, Devra drove to the heart of the matter. "What happened to you?"

"I was on my way back here. On foot, you know. It isn't far, and I fancy walking is good for me. Not too much walking, naturally. I knew a chap once, cousin of a friend of mine, who hurt himself quite badly walking —"

"You were on your way back here," said Devra, with a firmness of purpose that was not to be denied.

"Yes. And these two chaps stepped out of an alley and flanked me. Next thing I knew, I was jolly well *in* the alley, you know, and one of the chaps had knocked my hat off. 'I say!' I said. That had no effect on them, though. It was as if I hadn't spoken. I wonder if they were deaf? No, no, they weren't, and I'll tell you how I know: One of them said, 'Get that hat,' and the other one bent down to get it. That's when I tore myself out of the one chap's clutches and shoved the other chap out of the way and ran like billy-o! They'd have caught me, but a school had just let out and I sort of dodged amongst the students, you know, and got away. I went to ground: took cover until I was certain they had lost my scent."

Tambar Miznalia patted his arm approvingly until Holly suggested, "You didn't, by any chance, take cover overnight at Crossing the Bar?" Crossing the Bar was a notorious literature hang-out, frequented mainly by slim volumes of poetry.

"Needs must," said Three Men in a Boat (To Say Nothing of the Dog) in a martyred tone, by which he meant to say, "Yes."

"Well done," Devra admitted. "Did you know these ... chaps?"

"Never saw them before in my life. No, I tell a lie. I saw them once before, some little time ago, back when old Lolita did a bunk. Noticed them lurking about then. After Lolita didn't come back, it occurred to me they might have had something to do with it."

"Why didn't you say something at the time?" Constable Pel Darzin put the question, Devra and Holly being too busy controlling their tempers by counting to five-and-twenty.

"Well, it was only Lolita, you know, and I never did like that chap. Made one's skin crawl, didn't he? Book with a girl's name and a chap's narrative voice. Chap with the same name twice. Humbert Humbert? I mean, I say."

"Anything else you can tell us? Can you describe your assailants?" Pel Darzin pulled out a wireless device, soon to be obsolete when so many people had them it became common to call your mother and end up talking to a stripper on the other side of the globe. This time, he connected to his station house; he repeated the men's descriptions: Urban Wanderers in torn trousers and tunics with random words on them, one tall and blond with a silver chain around his neck, the other average in height and dark with blue stains on his teeth from eating raw jimjims.

Kurt Maxxon waited until the descriptions were transmitted, then asked, "Did you see them before any of your other library-mates' disappearances?" Showing that a good detective must tailor his questions to the person he's questioning, he added, "Think carefully."

Three Men in a Boat (To Say Nothing of the Dog) thought carefully. "No."

"Did they say anything?"

"One chap said, 'Get that hat.' Before that, just as they came out of the alley, the tall chap called me by name."

Holly asked, "Your personal name, or your title, or the name of your narrative character?" She was rather proud of that question. Constable Pel Darzin cast an admiring look her way.

"Oh! My title. I said yes, that was I. I offered to recite a sample. The bit where the three men try to open a tin of pineapple without a tin opener is always a favorite, but I never got the chance. They pushed me into the alley, and the struggle began."

Parlormaid Tambar Miznalia made one of those sounds that mean, *Oh, you poor, brave man! I'm so worried in retrospect!*

How wonderful you are! If you don't already know we're in love, this is putting you on official notice.

The Book looked at her with a besotted expression.

"I think that's your lot," Saradeeh told the investigators. "And looks like I might as well do laundry until the worst of this blows over."

Devra led the others into the hall. "Looks like any chance for fresh tea just went up the spout. Should we –"

Assistant Librarian Holly Jahangiri jumped and squeaked.

Kurt Maxxon patted her on the back and said, "Hold your breath and count to ten."

"That wasn't a hiccup," she said, stiffly, "it indicated a sudden insight."

"My mistake. What did you realize?"

"It might not mean anything, but all the missing works are in first person with a strong narrative voice."

Pel Darzin looked at Holly with hope written in every feature of his face. "You said it might not mean anything, but what *might* it mean?"

Such an appeal could not go unanswered. Holly thought hard and fast. "It might mean the kidnapper ... becomes attached to the narrative character and identifies that character with the Living Book and wants him or her exclusively?"

Kurt Maxxon proved his detective acumen by pointing out the flaws in this theory.

"But there are multiple Living Books of the same title. Are all copies of the same title disappearing?"

"No," Holly said. "Thank you ever so much for pointing out the flaw in my theory so quickly and easily."

Maxxon took a quick step away from her and said, "It's only by eliminating possibilities that we reach the best probability."

"Do another one, Assistant Librarian Holly Jahangiri," Darzin said.

"It might mean that the kidnapper becomes enamored of particular narrators. The persons narrating, I mean, rather than the characters narrating. And," she said, as another, more disturbing thought struck her, "there could be more than one kidnapper."

"Not impossible," Maxxon said.

Devra licked her thumb and touched it to her assistant's forehead in a sign of approval. "Not at all impossible. A great many people collect paper and digital volumes. Why shouldn't there be more than one collector of Living Books?"

Maxxon nodded. "How do we find them?"

Darzin's wireless phone buzzed and he answered the call. "Yes. Who? Of course. Understood."

As he tucked the device away, he said, "The men who tried to abduct Three Men In A Boat (To Say Nothing of the Dog) have been identified. They're low-level muscle men for Brax Distarta."

"The pratty baron?" Holly, being from the country, was well-acquainted with the name.

"That's the man. He's known to collect art, and he's suspected of dealing in stolen pieces. Also pratty rustling, though not in town, of course. We haven't been able to charge him with anything but, if we can pull him in for kidnapping, we can open the lid on his other clandestine activities."

"So," said Devra, "does this mean the constabulary is taking us seriously now?"

"It does, indeed," said Darzin. He took a notebook from his pocket and wrote down the time. "I'm on the clock. Pratty Baron Brax Distarta is in residence at his townhouse. A squad of detectives will be there directly. They've invited me to join them, as a courtesy. I'll let you know when we've made the arrest –"

A sound like a siren approached, and a little girl who seemed all pigtails and mouth pelted up to them.

"Pl'z, pl'ssm'n!" She clasped Darzin's tunic with both grubby hands.

Darzin looked around wildly, hoping to find another tablecloth before the urchin decided to blow her nose on his hem.

"Child," said Devra sternly, "this is a library. Modify your decibles."

The girl snuffled and wiped her face, nose included, on her pink over-tunic with the alley jammers printed on it. Holly recognized her as young Genesis Selinsky, oldest child of poor but honest library patrons. Her little brothers, Exodus and Leviticus, took most of their mother's attention, and Genesis sometimes ran the streets unsupervised.

"Now, child," said Devra. "What are you crying about?"

Having been chid, the girl switched directly from wail to mumble.

"...fr'en' ... o'n't ... Books ... I ... fah ... buh–" Her voice rose, in spite of herself– "TOOK 'EM!"

Holly, who majored in Library Science but minored in Childspeak, translated:

"She says a friend had an overnight. We pay triple-time for those; the poor Books read themselves hoarse. At any rate, this child followed them, planning to check them out as soon as they returned themselves, but somebody took them." She turned back to the child. "Can you describe the criminals?"

The little girl made more (to everyone but Holly) unintelligible sounds but, from her sketching a gesture that indicated a necklace and pointing to her teeth and gagging, they knew she was describing the men who had tried to abduct Three Men In A Boat (To Say Nothing of the Dog).

Holly said, "Thank you, little girl. Head Librarian Devra Langsam will see that you get some refreshment and a very large handkerchief."

"Delighted," said Devra, looking around for an underling to pass the child on to. Parlormaid Tambar Miznalia would be favorite.

"I'll be on my way, then," said Pel Darzin.

Kurt Maxxon put out a hand to restrain him. "I've got a stake in this. My friends disappeared into this man's hands. I want a part in bringing him to justice."

"I could deputize you...."

While they discussed this, Assistant Librarian Holly Jahangiri ducked into a nearby room and came out carrying three large guns. She tossed one to each of the men and checked to make sure her own was loaded with library-issue subcutaneous placator darts.

The constable shook his head. "Assis —"

"Don't tell me I'm not going." Holly's eyes glinted with rage. "They've taken *children's* Books! It's time to collect some overdues."

*

Kurt Maxxon had his souped-up pedicar parked outside and offered to drive. The three piled in and, before they could tie their seat belts, they were careening away at a breakneck thirty-five miles an hour.

Pel Darzin grasped the dash. "Can you handle it at this speed?"

Maxxon smiled grimly and steered around a goat. "Just give me directions, and I'll get us there."

Darzin directed Maxxon through the streets of Council City to an area where parks separated townhouses and mansions from one another, so the wealthy had the comfort of one another's company without the irritation of one another's presence.

"This one! Stop! Here!"

Maxxon slid to a smooth stop at the curb.

Darzin craned his neck, but saw no police cars nearby.

"They don't seem to have made it yet. We'll wait here —"

Holly was halfway to the door before Darzin began the second sentence.

"Assistant Librarian Holly Jahangiri! Wait for the detectives!"

"Not a chance," Holly snarled. "There are children's Books up there. Do you know what this man wants with them?"

"No."

"Neither do I. And he doesn't want us to know, or he'd check them out like any good citizen. Retired Detective Series Kurt Maxxon, you understand, don't you? You, of all people?"

Maxxon gave Darzin an apologetic look and joined Holly on the sidewalk.

"I do. I'm coming with you."

Darzin sighed and climbed out of the car. Antagonizing the biggest pratty baron in Meadow of Flowers district and flouting departmental protocol. That was two careers he could kiss goodbye.

Holly knocked at the door. A parlormaid who was as comfortably plump as Tambar Miznalia was annoyingly slender opened it. She was pale and wide-eyed, and clutched her apron in both hands.

"Oh!" She looked from one to the other of the three and stepped back. "Oh, thank goodness you've come! Them Books are downstairs in the rumpus room."

"Thank you, citizen," said Pel Darzin, as they filed past her. "Your cooperation is duly noted. Reinforcements are on the way. Please direct them to follow us."

"I will."

There was an awkward silence until Holly said, "Which way is the rumpus room?"

The parlormaid pointed to a door.

Pel Darzin and Kurt Maxxon bounced off each other,

trying to be the first into danger, leaving an opening for Holly to slip through and down the stairs.

At the bottom, she stopped, stunned at the sight before her. "Oh. Oh, my."

For the children's Books which had been kidnapped were A Series of Unfortunate Events: The Bad Beginning and The One Pig With Horns.

A Series of Unfortunate Events: The Bad Beginning had six men and four women in formal attire crowded into a corner. He recited himself to them while they listened, tears streaming down their faces.

The One Pig With Horns interspersed his narrative with costume and voice changes, sound effects and raging arguments with sock puppets. Three men and five women had barricaded themselves behind a table. When they saw the tunic of a constable, they raised their hands and competed with one another as to who could confess the loudest.

"The fools!" Holly beheld the carnage with pity and horror. "Don't they know children's Books are too strong for adults? Why do they think we keep them in a separate section?"

A clatter on the stairs was followed by a booming voice shouting, "Guilty parties on my right, innocents to my left! Look sharp, now!"

Holly leveled her subcutaneous placator pistol and opened fire. She caught A Series of Unfortunate Events: The Bad Beginning and lowered him gently to the floor. From that distance, she put another dart into the prone form of The One Pig With Horns, just to make sure he was well and truly placated.

*

Assistant Librarian Holly Jahangiri sat at a table in the lounge of the newly opened Jok'rel's Traveler's Rest Inn, sharing drinks with Sergeant Pel Darzin.

"Thanks to you," he said, "I'm on the fast track to detective. I'll be District Criminal Investigator one day."

"No one could deserve it more."

"All the Books have been found and returned to their libraries. The guilty parties have all confessed, demonstrated sincere remorse, and made reparations. But ... you were there when we debriefed the victim volumes. Did you understand what the criminals were doing?"

Holly, shoulders draped with her purple feather boa, took a deep draught of her drink, spitting the olive onto the floor, as etiquette demanded.

"They called them 'mash-ups'. They took two Books with strong, first-person narrative voices and forced them to recite themselves to one another simultaneously. It usually resulted in two ruined narratives, but sometimes they created a combination they considered entertaining. Those were rare and, to the illicit collectors, valuable. We've given those hybrids the option of renaming themselves and retaining their new content, and most of them are accepting that option. The rest of the spoiled works are either retiring or retraining themselves in their original texts."

Darzin shook his head, still befuddled by the concept.

Holly said, "I thought Retired Detective Series Kurt Maxxon was going to join us."

"He went back to his library to help his friends recover from their ... mashing up." He shifted uncomfortably, a shy flush tinting his cheeks. "I'm just as glad he couldn't make it, Assistant Librarian Holly Jahangiri."

*

Meanwhile, back at the library, Head Librarian Devra Langsam headed purposefully for the little librarian's room, the nearest place she could ditch Three Men In A Boat (To Say Nothing of the Dog). If Parlormaid Tambar Miznalia didn't talk him into marriage soon, she, Head Librarian Devra Langsam, would lose her mind.

"I say," he said, trailing her down the hall. "If I had one of those dog thingys, like the one in my book, he probably could have helped me fight those kidnap blighters off. Do you think you could get me one?"

"No."

"How about a swan?"

"No."

"A tin-opener?"

"No."

"A banjo?"

"VERY no."

The voices faded into the distance, and the hush of the library descended once again.

There's a Furry at the Bottom of My Garden, or, The Cat Who Fell to Earth

Andrea Gilbey

When I opened my bedroom curtains and saw that someone had dumped a shipping container at the bottom of my garden, I should have known that it was only the start. Okay, it wasn't actually *in* my garden, but it was butted right up to the wall on the other side, and have you seen the size of those things? You could live in one. Not the view you want from your back windows.

I ate a hurried breakfast, inwardly fuming, muttering all the while to my cats, Mungojerry and Rumpleteazer. And before you ask, no, I'm not a Lloyd Webber fan, I'm an Eliot fan.

After the usual futile button pressing exercise (why is there never an option to press for "none of the above"?), I finally managed to speak to a bored employee at the council offices who promised to send someone round to look at the container during the morning.

I work from home, so waiting in wasn't a problem, but looking out of my conservatory/work room at a rusting lump of blue metal was. I closed the blinds across the French doors and concentrated on writing instructions for my latest project for *Be Crafty* magazine.

The council official turned up just as I was about to start making my lunch, having given up on anyone ever coming. Clearly, the local officials have a looser definition of "morning" than I do.

Resplendent in a white hard hat, with an orange HiViz over

his dark suit, and unsuitably shod in shiny black Oxfords, the man from the council followed me down the side alley to the waste ground behind my house, tiptoeing around the puddles.

"So, this is the container that about which yourself contacted ourselves?" he asked. I blinked and mentally untangled the sentence. I felt like replying, "No, it's a spaceship from the planet Zuton," but held my tongue and nodded politely.

He flipped through a few sheets of paper on his clipboard, consulted a map and, with a mouth full of official jargon, informed me that, as the container was on a piece of land not coloured a pretty blue on his map, it did not fall under the council's remit.

"So, the council can't make whoever owns the land get rid of it?" I asked, folding my arms and wishing I'd put a cardigan on.

"It appears from the documentaryation that the deed of ownership of the said land lapsed within the requisite number of years, and therefore the land in question has no rightful owner," he convoluted.

"So, if no one owns the land, then I can call a haulage company to get rid of it? Obviously, I'll wait a while to see if anyone moves it first."

"Does legal right of egress onto this land belong to yourself or your property?" he asked.

"Err, I don't know. If no one owns the land, how can I find out?"

He snapped his pen shut with a flick and flapped the sheets on his clipboard back into place.

"Well, there you have the problem in an eggshell. Should you yourself need any further advice, please don't hesitate to contact ourselves. Oh, just one suggestion, how about a nice bit of trellis on the top of your wall? A clematoris would cover that in no time."

He turned and splodged his way back through the mud to his car, leaving me open-mouthed at his total lack of interest and his mangling of the English language.

*

I ate my lunch with my back to the window, thinking hard.

There were no shipping marks on the container, no labels to say who it belonged to, and it was securely sealed, so I couldn't find any information about the owner from the contents.

I would have to keep a watch on it and see if anyone appeared to remove whatever they were storing in it.

After lunch, I hauled my stepladder down to the bottom of the garden and propped it by the wall. The ground was uneven and the ladder wobbled as I climbed to the top and balanced myself against the bricks to measure the amount of container sticking up above the wall. This thing was huge; it would take a piece of trellis at least as high again as the wall itself to hide it from view, let alone a "clematoris."

Backing down off the ladder, I stepped on something hard, which felt as though it had stabbed through the sole of my plastic gardening clog and into my foot. The day was just getting better and better.

I bent to look for the offending stabby article and found a small rectangle of metal, about a centimetre thick and the size of a credit card. On one side, it was embossed with a swirling design that appeared to be random, and on the reverse, there were raised sections in various shapes, like 1970s Scandinavian art pottery. The metal itself was a strange dull blue, which looked as though it had been annealed in some way.

Limping indoors to tend to my bruised foot, I slipped the object into my pocket; it might come in useful as inspiration for a craft project.

*

I spent the afternoon planning patchwork blocks for a Christmas table runner project – odd in April, but that's the wonderful world of craft publications for you – and immersed myself in fabric swatches to take my mind off the eyesore at the bottom of the garden. It wasn't until darkness fell and I was about to close the blinds that I remembered it.

I decided to leave the conservatory window unshaded so that if anyone approached the container with a torch, or if car headlights shone across the waste ground, I would see it immediately.

No one came the whole evening, and I gathered up the cats and headed to bed, resigned to waking up again with the blue monstrosity in full view.

Other people have fairies at the bottom of their garden.[1]

*

I woke in the night a few times, unsure what had startled me out of sleep. The cats were curled up on the bed snoring and twitching in their dreams. The fourth time I woke, I was sure I had heard scraping metal. I gently moved a tangle of furry legs and eased my way out of bed, twitching the curtains apart slightly to peer into the night. There was no sign of a light on the waste ground, and it was too dark to see if anyone was moving around out there.

I slid back into bed and fell into an unsettled doze for the remaining few hours.

*

The next morning the stray cat arrived.

*

I was washing my breakfast bowl and thinking about making another pot of coffee when I noticed the cat. It was sitting upright on the edge of the raised herb bed outside the kitchen window, apparently sound asleep. It wasn't an animal I had seen before: it was so unusual looking I would have remembered it.

Its face was long, with high cheekbones, like a Siamese, but its coat was more like a Persian in texture, rippling from the

---

[1] The allusion is to a comedy song made famous by Beatrice Lilley – also a reference to someone who is vague and dreamy.

ruff around its neck along its back and down its legs and tail, and stirring in the light breeze. The most original thing about it was its colouring. Its fur was a dark chocolate brown at the roots, shaded through a rich tawny bronze to white at the very tips, almost as though it had been to the hairdresser for an ombré tint which had gone slightly wrong.

It opened its eyes and I gasped. One eye was golden yellow and the other a limpid emerald green, but it was the expression in the eyes that struck me – an expression so deep and full of worldly sorrow that it brought tears to my eyes.

The cat looked well cared for: its coat was sleek and in good condition, but it wouldn't hurt to just offer it a tiny treat, would it?

I opened the kitchen door slowly, checking behind me to make sure that my two boys were nowhere in sight: at that time of the morning they were usually asleep in a patch of sunlight on my bed.

The strange cat turned its head as I opened the door, gave me a long, slow, eye-squeeze greeting, then jumped down and scuttled straight past me into the house.

I ran after it, trying to race it to the door that separated the kitchen from the rest of the house, but it was too fast for me and shot down the hallway.

Great. A strange cat in the house; from what I had seen of its back view as it flashed past, an intact male; about to start a fight with my two, who were snoozing peacefully.

I hurried up the stairs, trying to step quietly so as not to scare Mungo and Rumps, and listening for sounds of fighting. I peered cautiously into my bedroom, expecting to see at best arched backs and glaring, and at worst a seething ball of fur, teeth and claws, but there were my boys, side by side on the bed in the sunshine, busily and noisily washing each other's ears.

The intruder was sitting on a chair at the bottom of the bed, watching with narrowed eyes, but there was no sense of antagonism or even acknowledgement between the cats; it was as though Mungo and Rumps couldn't see the interloper.

I approached the cat on the chair, cautiously, but remembering the eye-squeeze greeting, and held my hand out to be sniffed. The stranger's eyes flashed as he hissed, and lashed out with a paw, catching my knuckles and drawing blood.

I gasped in shock and pain and withdrew my hand. The cats on the bed continued grooming each other as though nothing had happened.

"Hey, you two, how about defending your human a little bit, hmm?" I reached for a tissue to dab my cuts.

Mungo and Rumps turned their heads together, looked at me with their identical green and gold-ringed eyes, and carried on washing.

"Thanks for everything, boys, remind me to do the same for you some time," I muttered.

Grabbing a pillow as a shield I prodded the strange cat from behind until, hissing, he jumped sulkily from the chair and ran downstairs. Closing the bedroom door behind me, I headed to the bathroom to disinfect my wounds.

Downstairs, all was quiet. The visitor had bolted outside through the open back door.

*

I settled down to work in the conservatory and, absorbed as I was in my project, it was nearly one thirty before I looked up and saw the strange cat sitting silently by the French doors, staring at me solemnly. Most cats avoid prolonged eye contact, but the eyes of this odd creature never wavered from mine. There was something weirdly un-catlike about its stare. I shivered uneasily and looked away, and, the spell broken, the cat ran down the garden.

*

In a flash of multi-coloured fur, he leapt onto the wall, and with another mighty bound was on top of the container. He shook himself to fluff up his fur and settled down in tea-cozy pose on the top of the eyesore. That big expanse of metal was probably nice and warm in the sunshine.

I turned to the stove to make some lunch.

The water for my pasta hadn't yet come to the boil when the noise started outside.

"Mraaaaow, owww, owww, owww. Ohhhhmmmmraaooo-wwwwwww, wrowww wowww owwww!"

The cat was pacing up and down on top of the container, occasionally stopping to scratch at the corners, and singing the mournful song of his people.

I tried to ignore the racket and make my lunch in peace, but it was hard going.

This was just getting better and better – first a hunk of junk gets dumped at the end of my garden, then I get a visiting cat who thinks he's Pavarotti.

Amazingly, there was no reaction from my peacefully dozing moggies upstairs, but the cacophony was getting on my nerves long before the last mouthful of spag bol. I bolted the last few strands without tasting them and threw the bowl into the sink.

Snatching up a spare feeding bowl from the cupboard, I flung open the kitchen door and banged the empty bowl against the wall outside. The way things were going so far, the contrary animal would probably think it was a call for food, but with any luck it would shut him up.

It worked.

With a final strangled "Mraaow" he jumped down from the container and vanished. Quietly.

Sensing that all was peaceful for a while, Mungo and Rumps trotted down the stairs and rubbed around my ankles. It was hours until they were due more food, but as it had been such a strange morning, I decided to indulge them and split a sachet of salmon and courgette Felix between their bowls.

I gathered up an armful of washing from the laundry basket and stuffed it into the machine. Something heavy and hard fell to the floor with a clunk as I closed the machine door and pressed the start button. It was the rectangle of metal that I'd picked up in the garden the day before; I must have left it in my jeans pocket. I carried it through to the conservatory and slid it into the drawer of my work table that I kept for what I called "treasures": found items that may come in useful as inspiration.

The cats followed me, in playful mood, so I gathered up some of their toys and raced them into the sitting room for playtime. Work could wait.

*

When I finally looked up from the pattern I was drafting, it was getting dark outside. Seven o'clock already. I tidied my equipment on the desk and flipped open the laptop for one last check of my inbox before finishing work for the day. Corrections and questions on some pattern instructions from one of the magazine's test crafters awaited a reply, but I could answer that in the morning.

I shut down the computer and turned out the lights, intending to spend a cozy evening in the sitting room watching TV with a cat or two curled up on my lap, and maybe a glass of wine.

I had almost forgotten about the stray, until the scratching started at the kitchen door.

There he was, looking up through the window, proudly offering me a very dead vole.

"Sorry, my lovely, but I don't really fancy that: it's very kind of you to offer, but I think I prefer pizza. Want some? We could send out?"

He looked at me steadily, with the dead vole hanging either side of his mouth like a limp moustache, then dropped it and uttered a sharp, "Maoow!"

"Oh, so you don't fancy mouldy vole, either? I don't blame you. Let's see what's we can find for you, shall we?"

I opened the back door, slid through before the cat had a chance to realise his opportunity, and dropped a few cat treats by his feet, carefully not approaching too closely.

He sniffed them, licked one, picked it up delicately between his teeth and crunched it, then politely turned away and vomited on the tiles.

I sighed, hoping the visitor wasn't about to become ill. If he wouldn't even let me touch him, there was no way I could pick him up to take him to a vet without being shredded to ribbons.

Having rid himself of whatever had upset his stomach, he sat and watched me clean up his offerings, his eyes narrowed, the tip of his tail twitching from side to side. I kept up a calm, low voiced stream of nonsense chatter to reassure him, being careful not to put any part of myself too close to those needle-sharp claws.

"There, all tidy." I looked up at an empty space where a cat had been.

Vanished again.

"I think I'll call you Macavity," I muttered to the gathering dusk. "You appear and create chaos, then suddenly you're not there."

Did I imagine a pair of shining eyes watching me intently from beneath the viburnum?

*

The second movement of the concerto for cat and container started at around two a.m. This time the vocals were accompanied by the screech of claws on metal. It sounded as though the cat were wearing steel tipped gloves – surely those little claws couldn't make that much noise?

I tossed and turned for a while, amazed once more that my own cats were sleeping through the racket, but after half an hour of eardrum abuse I had to do something.

I slipped out of bed and opened the window wide.

"SHUT. UP!"

The yowling and scraping stopped abruptly and a large shadow, highlighted against a full moon, slithered down from the rectangular block and vanished into the darkness. Amazing how much bigger things can look in silhouette.

I crawled back into bed and pulled the pillows over my head.

*

The following day dawned with no sign of my operatic friend, and the three of us breakfasted in peace.

I needed to go shopping, so I gathered purse and bags, checked the litter tray, and hunched into my raincoat. Latching the front gate behind me, I decided to risk the mud in the alley and check on the container once more. Nothing appeared to be any different until I looked up. Then, with a shiver, I noticed large scratches around the top of the box, much too big to be a cat's claw marks. Someone had been trying to break into the thing.

I hurried away, glancing nervously behind me. What was in there? Why had it been dumped where it was? And who was desperate to get at the contents, apart from the stray cat?

Maybe it was a consignment of tuna that had "fallen off the back of a lorry." Or catnip? Why else would the cat be obsessed with the thing?

*

I let the shopping bags slump against the wall and dropped my keys on the hall table.

Something was wrong – someone was in the house: I just knew. The atmosphere felt wrong – occupied, somehow.

The cats! Where were my babies?

A little face appeared between the banisters and the two animals padded down the stairs to greet me as they always did when I came home. Maybe I was wrong. Could the other cat have climbed through a window I'd forgotten to close? Was it his presence I thought I could sense?

I fussed over Mungo and Rumps, giving myself some thinking time, then shooed them upstairs and closed the hall door. I grabbed a golf umbrella from the hall stand and grasped the handle of the sitting room door. Silently I counted to three, then flung the door open, umbrella held like a pike, ready to charge.

Sitting in the armchair, his legs curled under him, hands rested calmly in his lap, eyes closed, was a man.

In a split second my brain took in his appearance: slim, probably tall, I judged from the way he was folded into the chair; very pale skin; dressed in a simple white shirt and dark trousers.

It was his hair that caught my attention, falling in a heavy bob to his shoulders, dark at the roots, then shaded through auburn to white at the tips.

I couldn't decide whether to attack him with the umbrella or ask him for the name of his hairdresser.

"Hey, what the hell do you think you're doing in my house?"

I aimed the metal ferrule of the umbrella at the centre of his chest and shouted at him, trying to sound more confident than I felt. "Don't move, keep your hands in your lap, don't try anything funny."

Why hadn't I thought to grab my phone out of my raincoat pocket?

He opened his eyes slowly and gazed at me. Those eyes! One golden, one green, and with weirdly almond shaped pupils.

He sat motionless, apparently processing the sight of the irate woman in front of him.

"I mean you no harm."

His voice was low but rich, with a strange rumble deep in his throat, and he spoke as one speaking a foreign language learned from a book.

"Who are you, and what are you doing in my house? How did you get in?"

The umbrella stayed poised at "charge."

Again, the stillness, as though he was analysing my questions.

"You let me in yesterday, quite willingly, so I saw no harm in returning."

"I let you…? When was that, exactly? No one has been here except the council man, and he didn't come in the house. Who are you?"

"Your tongue cannot sound my true name, but yesterday you named me Macavity."

After a few moments, I remembered to close my mouth.

"Oh, right, so you're a cat, are you? How silly of me not to recognise you," I laughed scornfully, keeping the umbrella poised.

He somehow shimmied in the chair and for a split second I saw my feline visitor of the day before, curled on the cushion.

I blinked.

"Okay, how did you do that?"

He blinked in his turn, slow and thoughtful.

"My transponder cannot find the words in your speech to explain."

"Your trans*whater*? Are you trying to tell me you're some kind of alien? A being from outer space?"

"Correct."

"You're … a space cat. Okay, I'll go along with it. So, where's your space ship? Hmm?"

He paused, thinking. This would be good. I rested the umbrella against the wall and folded my arms. What I had here was a nutter. Maybe a dangerous nutter, but for the moment I felt quite safe. Let him spin his story.

"My craft experienced a fuel leak, and I was forced to make an emergency landing at the rear of your domicile."

I was starting to believe in this transponder, I wasn't sure what volume of the dictionary it was working from, circa 1890, perhaps?

"I used what was left of the ship's energy to create a guising force field. As I flew over the periphery of your land I saw many stationary vehicles of a rectangular shape, so I used this design as a pattern."

"You ... parked your ... spaceship at the bottom of my garden? And turned it into a *container?*" I shouted the last word.

He reacted oddly to my anger; another shimmy, and for a moment I thought I saw a huge, beautiful, muscular cat-like beast standing before me on its hind legs, canine teeth bared, eyes blazing.

I shuddered and took a step back. Breathe. Just breathe, you're seeing things.

"I beg your pardon, my energy grows weak the longer I am on this world and close to humans, and I cannot always control my guising. Please do not fear me. I need your help."

He looked at me with an intense gaze. He sounded so pathetic. It could be a trap, but ... I shook my head as if to clear my brain. I was starting to believe this rigmarole!

Slowly, I sat down on the sofa at angles to the chair, watching for the slightest movement from the intruder.

"So. You want me to help you re-fuel your ... spaceship?"

"Any fuel on this backward world would destroy it. I need to gain entry to the ship so I may repair my communication system. Fuel will be sent."

Sent? How?

"So, you've locked yourself out?"

"I have mislaid the ... handle ... to my ship." He sounded uncertain of the word.

Handles. OK, we could find him a handle, if that's all it would take to get rid of him.

"Stay there. Do not move. Do not touch anything. Understand?"

He stared, blinked, and tilted his head to one side.

"I'll take that as a yes."

Closing the door behind me, I scuttled into the conservatory and collected my laptop, running a search for handles as I walked back, not to waste a second in getting rid of him.

"Handles. There." I turned the screen towards him, trying to make my shaky hands hold still.

He gave a superior smile.

"My great-grandsire told me that there were worlds where people still used such primitive technology."

"Look, do you want me to help you or not?" Anger momentarily overcame my fear and disbelief.

He bowed his head, which I interpreted as an apology of sorts.

I pulled a stool up near his chair, but not too close, and scrolled through photos of handles, but he shook his head at every one.

Scrolling on, with a thudding pulse that surely he could hear, I spoke with an assumed calmness. "So, how do you communicate, then? Telepathically?"

"Of course," he replied, matter-of-factly.

"Okay." I glanced sideways at him. "No thumbs, right?"

He looked blankly at me, so I searched for a cat-meme about how cats would take over the world if they only had thumbs.

Blank stare again.

"It's a joke. You know? Humour? Ha ha? Oh, never mind."

I felt just the way I always did if I made a joke or did a silly voice to the cats and they looked blankly at me.

I flipped the laptop closed; we were getting nowhere.

"Come on, there's a hardware shop down the road, we'll go and see what handles they have." Boldly, I tapped him on the arm. Ow! A tingle shot up through my hand. That was some serious static he had going on.

He hissed, flinching away and hunching into himself as if in severe pain, his face even paler than before.

"I'm sorry! It was just a tap. I…"

He calmed himself, panting a little, mouth slightly open, blinking slowly.

"Please, do not touch me. Human contact weakens my already depleted strength."

He looked at me with such pain in his eyes that I almost wanted to hug him better, but if what he said was true, that would probably kill him. Or me.

"Okay. No contact, understood," I said, shakily.

How had I gone from encountering a suspected burglar to believing in this alien story and feeling sympathy for him? At least if I could get him out of the house to the hardware shop I could keep him out. Better shut that upstairs window over the conservatory first, though, or he would just climb back in.

*

The assistant in the hardware shop looked askance at my strange companion, but said nothing, and brought us box after box of handles, but each was received and rejected sadly.

Light suddenly dawned. Idiot that I was! We needed a handle for a car, or some kind of vehicle, not a house door handle.

I shepherded my charge down the road to a branch of Halfords and we looked through more boxes of car and van door handles, but still no recognition.

Macavity followed me back home. I didn't know what else to do with him; I couldn't just abandon him, and he seemed so depressed at not finding a suitable handle. He was walking badly, shuffling along with a pained expression on his face.

As I unlocked the door I heard a hissing gasp behind me and turned in alarm to see the huge, magnificent cat-like creature that I had glimpsed earlier towering over me, odd-coloured eyes flashing, back arched, multi-hued fur rippling.

With an obvious effort, he faded back to human form, his face looking more drained and in pain than ever. Clearly, he was finding it harder by the minute to shift his shape as his energy wore down. Quite possibly my presence was making him weaker, although I was careful not to touch him or be too close to him, for more reasons than one.

"That! That is what I mislaid. The handle!"

I looked down at the bunch of metal objects in my hand.

Trying not to show how shaken I was at his transformation I replied, "I think your transponder software needs updating, kitty cat, those are *keys*, not handles!"

At least we were getting closer.

*

"Maybe you dropped the key in my garden? Or on the waste ground at the back? Maybe it's still out there. Let's go and look."

He dragged himself slowly to the back door. I could hardly bear to watch him; the pain in his eyes was so intense, and every few seconds a shudder passed through him and showed a glimpse of the real creature under the disguise. With a sigh, he allowed himself to become the cat that I had first met – was it only two days earlier? Communicating with him would be harder, but he seemed to find being a small feline easier than being a human.

I scanned the garden, inch by inch, while Macavity sat wearily on the raised bed, watching me intently.

"Could you draw the key for me? If you can turn back to human again?"

He strained, shoulders hunched. A faint hint of the human, then gone again. His strength was waning fast.

"Maybe we can pick the lock! Let me see what tools I've got in my desk drawer."

I rummaged in the drawer, pulling things out and scattering them across the desk top. Macavity followed me indoors and jumped painfully onto the desk to watch. The odd metal object I had found in the garden clunked onto the desk, and Macavity sat upright, the pupils of his eyes growing large. He stretched out a paw and tapped at the object, hitting it closer and closer to the edge of the desk.

Crossly, I pushed it back again.

Tap, tap tap.

"Look, this isn't the time to play kitty-cat games, I'm trying to help you here."

Tap, tap, tap, clunk.

I bent to pick up the object and found my face level with a pair of intently staring eyes. I slowly placed the thing in front of him and he gently rested a paw on it in a gesture of ownership, claws gripping the edge.

"This? This is your key?"

He looked at me and blinked slowly, purring softly between pained breaths.

I stared at him for a moment. Suddenly the thought of him leaving caused me a jolt of pain. I straightened my shoulders and stood up.

"Come on, then, let's do this."

I picked up the key and stepped into the garden, leading the way out through the side gate and down the alley to the waste ground and the container.

I studied the high metal walls; where was the lock? Hidden under the … force field or whatever he had created around his vehicle.

I looked down at the exhausted cat, helpless to know what to do.

He squeezed his eyes shut, with an intense look of concentration on his face, and managed, with an effort that took most of his remaining strength, to transform once more into human form. I rubbed the sleeve of my jumper across the key, to try to remove as much human taint as possible, and held it out to him so he could grasp the farthest corner.

He reached a stiff arm out and gripped the edge of the object between fingers and thumb, his eyes never leaving mine. The jolt of pain that shot through him when he grasped the key was like an electric shock, transmitted through the metal and coursing up my arm.

For a second, we held the thing between us, eyes locked, each barely breathing, then I slowly lowered my arm.

He placed the object gently in his mouth and seemed to relax into his true form. Drained as he was, he was still the most beautiful and terrifying beast I have ever seen or probably ever will, a larger, wilder, more vital version of the cat that had appeared from nowhere two days earlier.

His eyes glowed and the container was surrounded by a sudden shivering silver light. I turned away, momentarily dazzled. When I looked back he was gone, taking the light with him. I was standing in a muddy field in front of a rusty old shipping container, feeling as though all the energy had been sucked out of me.

*

It must have been at least five minutes before I was able to move, and even then, I lingered for a while, listening. There was no sound from inside the container.

I trailed slowly indoors and trod heavily upstairs to find my cats.

"You boys have no idea what's being going on, have you?" I asked as I sat between them on my bed, rubbing their warm, round little heads. "You didn't even see that other cat, did you? You must think Mama's lost her marbles, hmm? Maybe I have! Maybe I put some of your catnip in my dinner last night instead of herbs, eh? That would explain a lot."

They butted their heads against me and purred, seeming to understand that I needed comforting. I felt no inclination to do any work, so I made a strong, sweet cup of milky tea and subsided into an armchair in the front room, with a cat either side of me on the arms, chirruping and nuzzling my shoulders.

I felt drained and blank and have no idea how long I sat,

staring into space and thinking about nothing. When I finally realised that it was getting dark, I also discovered that I was hungry, having eaten nothing since breakfast.

I was reluctant to venture into the kitchen, knowing what the object in full view of its window now contained, but I wasn't going to find food anywhere else, so I made myself walk the few steps and inspect the view. There was nothing beyond the garden wall except distant trees and sky. Gone.

I flopped into a chair, feeling weirdly empty, trying to understand my feelings for this ... creature ... who had appeared and disappeared, leaving behind such conflicting emotions.

*

The cats followed me into the kitchen in hopes that I might accidentally spill some more food into their bowls, and Mungo called me to attention with his quiet, questioning, "Ma-aa-aaow?"

I turned and looked at the two little animals, so sweet and easy to love. I knelt between them and scratched their ears and chins as they purred and nuzzled against me.

"Well, then, boys," I murmured into their soft fur as I kissed their heads, none of us understanding the warm tears that ran down my face. "He's gone. It's over. Macavity's not there."

Cat Power
J. Baumgartle

Humans are very slow. I ought to know. I've been training mine since I was a kitten and still find it necessary to supplement my diet with an occasional bird or mouse. The flexible portal from the kitchen to the out-of-doors has long been my recourse to a more varied menu. It also enables me to fulfill the nocturnal mandates of a three-year-old adult male.

It isn't as if I were alone in this small, sleepy neighborhood. Cat residents and strays alike visit the oak they know is mine. They gauge my mood by the height of the branch I've chosen and climb as far as my approval permits. We understand each other and negotiate our positions at will. A poor climber will be tolerated, but an aggressive one will not.

Veva, my human, goes quietly about her day and even notices me on occasion. But if I weren't sharing my house with her, I'm not sure how she would manage. She is afraid of mice, panics if a bird comes in through an open window, and runs outside while shouting into her cell phone. When help arrives to show the creature the way out, she moans with gratitude, fearfully reenters the house, and plops down on the couch, exhausted. To be fair, she is showing some age.

I do worry that her sleep habits are inconsistent with sunrise and sunset. Though I attempt with all gentleness to begin her day with the rising sun, so that she can incorporate a reasonable number of naps before dark, she merely feeds me and goes back to bed. I believe her to have been reared somewhat carelessly, though with affection. Certainly, with affection.

Veva sings to me and tells me stories while I sit on her lap. The stories make no sense, but my purring seems to comfort her; so I listen and watch the curved wood under the chair tilt back and forth.

Outside, someone hits the door three times. We jump and rush to see who it is. It's *that* man again. He hands Veva a clipboard with a dangling pen, then takes us to the tall oak near the limbless pole. My oak. Dirty machines and dusty men pause there while he continues to talk in his perfunctory manner. He speaks to her in a tone that has no yielding to it: rudeness, in my own front yard. I feel my tail bristle and turn my ears back, to let him know this is not acceptable.

My human stands there shaking her head; the scent of distress surrounds her. The man's focus suddenly lights on me, and as I leap at him with outstretched claws, he kicks at me, displacing enough air to convince me to scramble up my tree to avoid being crushed. As I hunker there, trembling, I am surprised to hear Veva raising a commotion. The out-faced man, and his fellows, grudgingly mount their machines and go away. That evening, Veva spends a lot of time using her cell phone. I want to help, but she has to come to me. When she does, and we sit together, I feel I am more than just a last resort.

*

The next morning starts out noisily. Machines pull onto the grass before Veva is even awake. At the foot of the oak I crouch, hissing a stance, defying these dirty humans. They make sounds that wheedle and ply, which aggravates me no end. Veva runs out of the house in her bathrobe, prepared to put herself at risk, and I let out a yowl. There is a brief silence while all parties consider the situation. Meanwhile, I have found a good limb from which to leap. The man pulls a string on a metal contraption which whirrs like the end of the world. My human pleads with him, then turns to me, coaxing me to come down. Now, though, it is a point of honor to defend my position.

After a red-faced stretch of intense silence, that dog-breath man backs off and stomps toward his machines, and I am pleased to say that those people move on. Of course, they may double back, or return with reinforcements, for all the good it will do them.

A long evening and longer night ensues, but I am still here when the machines arrive, just before daylight. In answer to the deafening whirr below my tree, I yowl, over and over as if I were being declawed, and by ones and twos, the feline population of this valley insinuate their way up my tree, hissing and snarling and spitting at any advance of the men. We arrange ourselves into a tree full of eyes, glaring into the almost day. The men don't yield and neither do we. Whatever happens, we're in it now.

The stalemate continues as a work-booted Veva makes an appearance, pointing, and showing her cell phone, as more people arrive to see what's happening. Her speech and gestures seem to make a difference. Finally, the unlimbed pole is taken down and restrung in its new position across the road. The oak has been saved. We sing our victory.

My human seems to have spilled an entire bag of cat food over the ground, which will certainly not go to waste.

Humans: Herders or Herdees?

Janet Wolanin Alexander

Dream on, Two-Leggeds! You may well fancy yourselves as the herders; but we four-leggeds, especially we cats, know better.

*

Shadow, 1993-2009. I was a brown-eyed, short-haired black beauty that my first human, a university prof, named Lady Macbeth. When he passed away, his family dropped me off at the biology office in hopes of rehoming me. I was huddled in a back corner of a large dog crate, trying very hard to appear regal, when Jim walked in. I immediately enchanted him.

Jim took me to his apartment after work. I followed him everywhere, including onto his bed where I spent the first night. Jim renamed me Shadow for my endearing tracking and snuggling skills.

A while later, Jim introduced me to his girlfriend, Jan, a teacher in charge of a school garden. Around Halloween, the Js took me to the pumpkin patch for a photo shoot. I modeled beautifully against the orange background of an especially large Jack-o-lantern-to-be.

The couple got married in August. As soon as the three of us moved into our new apartment, I immediately made myself indispensable to Jan. Whenever she lay on the couch, I climbed onto her stomach and mesmerized her with my petite perfection. She contemplated me as a study in geometry, especially triangles, à la nature artist Charles Harper. And, when she lay in bed with a sore back, I sat on the spot warming it way better than any electric heating pad could.

At dinner, I jumped onto my chair and sat, my head peeking just above the table. I looked back and forth as the Js conversed. Sometimes they took turns pretending to speak for me in funny voices.

One day, Jim wondered aloud if I were lonely, being home alone so much. Jan overheard.

*

Midnight, 1996–2014. While shopping at the pet store, Jan noticed me among the feline orphans up for adoption by a rescue organization. A young, long-bodied short-hair, I'd come from a racetrack where, according to the volunteer, superstitions about black cats abound and I wouldn't have survived very long. When Jan's baby blues met my gorgeous greens, I was chosen as Shadow's sister.

Jan went through a pretty rigorous process to become my foster mom. She described my prospective home, promised to keep me indoors, and supplied references. They were checked, her application was approved, and I was taken home as an early Christmas surprise for Jim. When he saw me, his blue-greys lit right up!

At first, Shadow and I were kept on opposite sides of the apartment with our own belongings. Soon, some items were switched so we could whiff each other's scent. Then we were put in adjoining rooms where we could sniff each other under the door. When we were finally paired, it was under the Js' supervision for increasing lengths of time. It didn't take Shadow and me long to share litter boxes and demonstrate that we could be safely left together during the day. I was easy to get along with – an introvert who preferred keeping to myself.

Renters in our apartment complex were charged a pet fee. When Jan went to the office to pay mine, she was told that, due to the *strict* one-pet-per-apartment rule, she and Jim had to get rid of me or move out. This came as a surprise as two dogs lived in the apartment below ours. Rather than making a fuss, however, the Js decided it was time to buy a house and bought one from friends. I was a good luck cat!

*

Hobbes, 2000–2012. One weekend, the friends heard an animal whimpering in pain outside their new house. They found me lying injured under a bush. They figured I'd been hit by a car and called the Js who drove right over. Jan carefully picked me up and held me in her lap while Jim drove a long way to a 24/7 emergency animal hospital because the local veterinary clinics were closed.

The Js had to make an important decision before I could be cared for: they either had to adopt me and promise to pay my medical expenses, or give me up, leaving my fate to the veterinarian who wouldn't disclose it to them. Fortunately, I'd totally smitten Jan; and Jim, afraid I'd be euthanized, wanted to give me a fighting chance. I became their expensive cat. Jim named me after his favorite cartoon feline, the one in Bill Watterson's *Calvin and Hobbes.*

X-rays revealed that one of my legs was badly broken and surgery might not save it. The needed operation was too expensive there at the hospital, so my leg was stabilized and I was medicated and sent home. After a few days of living in a crate in a quiet room, a more affordable surgeon operated on me. My leg wasn't amputated, and, after it healed, I walked again with nary a limp!

Shadow and Midnight didn't care at all for going outdoors on walks with Jan and Jim – they froze when buckled into harnesses – but I was so happy to walk again that I didn't need one. I loved strolling down the sidewalk with the Js and visiting the neighbors.

I was a sight to behold – a large, laid-back, gentle giant and a very handsome, long-haired, yellow-and-white Maine

Coon with an immaculate white bib and socks. Speaking of socks, I especially charmed them off lady humans and, in no time, had a fan club going!

Indoors, my favorite activity was watching the fish in the aquarium. The Js dubbed it "watching the Fish Channel on Cat TV."

I liked Shadow and Midnight okay, but yearned for a brother, too.

*

Calvin, 2002-2013. I was a youngster crying on the edge of a cornfield when a long line of bicyclists passed by on the road. The Js stopped and found me. While Jan tried to keep hold of me, Jim rode his bike back to their car. I wriggled in Jan's arms with all my might. Strong and healthy, I had almost tired her out when the house owner across the street came over and gave her permission to contain me in his shed until Jim returned.

Jim named me Calvin after cartoon Hobbes's mischievous buddy. A bundle of energy, I provided the Js with endless entertainment. I jumped from floor to furniture and long distances from piece to piece. I slept around – in the bathroom sink, on the lid of the picnic basket, on top of the TV and refrigerator, in laps and on beds, etc. Speaking of beds, I loved it when Jan made them – I darted under the fresh sheets as they floated down and slithered like a mole under the blankets, daring her to grab me as I tunneled quickly around.

My favorite antic was climbing door frames. The Js don't believe in declawing and I enthusiastically repaid them by fashionably distressing the woodwork.

I was a handsome, black-and-white short-hair, a butterfly more social than Shadow. Once, after the Js had passed out slices of ice cream cake at a birthday party, they left the unclaimed piece on the counter. I jumped up, sampled some frosting, and then launched to the top of the refrigerator to survey the action. All of a sudden, I felt ill and bazooka barfed blue frosting across the room. (Fortunately, no guest was hit.)

Unlike my doppleganger-to-to come, I was a friendly trouble maker.

*

Cookie, 2000-present. No one knew that another black-and-white cat was living outside the house – until the snowy afternoon that Jim discovered me under the plastic tarp that covered the deck swing and took me inside. I'm a looker: the feline counterpart of a female Pepé Le Pew, a gorgeous Ragdoll with long, soft hair, permanent black "eye-liner" extending from my lids, and a long, fluffy tail. I'm more than eye candy, however; I'm also a hissy, street-smart spitfire who knows how to use her weapons, and I immediately claimed the diva-ship of the Js' clowder. I'm not afraid of the other cats, the dogs, or even the Js, who gave me the stupid name Cookie because of my Oreo colors. I indulge their petting when so inclined, but also keep their reflexes sharp, as I can change my mind in a blink! Too bad, so sad, for everyone in the house, especially the next adoptee.

*

Grayce, 2009-present. One afternoon, the Js' block-watch captain emailed the neighborhood that I'd strayed onto her front porch and had to go ASAP because of her kids' allergies. Because no one jumped at the opportunity and my declawed front paws disabled me from defending myself in the wild, Jan brought over a carrier and took me home.

Jan is not a fan of cutesy spellings, so I am surprised by the Y she inserted into my name.

Physique-wise, I am a gray version of Shadow – a small, petite, perfectly proportioned, female short-hair who effortlessly maintains her youthful figure.

Cookie may be everyone's diva, but I'm the Js' boss. If they aren't up when I want breakfast, I jump on them and meow incessantly. When I want out of a closed room, I thump on the door until they open it. At bedtime I follow them into the bathroom and insist that they turn on a faucet. Drinking from a bowl on the floor at night – how gauche!

Like Cookie, I only lap sit when and where I choose and I don't like being picked up. Whenever a J tries to remove me from a place where I've settled, I, too, protest. My tactic for getting what I want? Wearing the Js down – it pains me to say – with my *dogged* determination.

Soon, Shadow and Midnight and Calvin and Cookie weren't going to be the only sets of "color twins"; I was going to get a "twin" of my own.

*

Brooke, 2010-present. Jan was outside with the dogs one night when she heard me mewing plaintively. Flashlight in hand, she climbed the fence and stepped onto the creek bank. Her slow sweeping finally spotlighted me: a tiny kitten all alone. As Jan stepped toward me, I skedaddled into a crevice in a pile of cement blocks. Jan bravely reached in and extracted me. With me in one hand and her flashlight in her mouth, she carefully climbed back over the fence.

Another gray, female short-hair, I was housed for several weeks at the kennel/grooming salon where Jan works. Her hope was that another employee or a customer would adopt me; none did, so she took me home and named me after the place we met.

I've grown from a tiny babe into an adult so large that Jan grunts when she picks me up. The vet says I need to lose weight, but I like to finish off the food the others leave in their bowls.

I'm usually low maintenance and laid-back. Right now, however, I'm jealous of the attention Jan is paying the computer. I'm trying to distract her by rubbing and bumping her legs, standing on my hind ones, putting my front ones on her chair, and purring loudly. Eventually, she stops and pets me. Not long enough, though, so I jump onto the desk and poke my cold nose into her left ear, sit on her paper, and rake her hair with a front paw. She keeps typing. I drop to the floor and renew my rubbing and bumping. In desperation, I give her a love nip and, like a dog, roll onto my back and expose my fat tummy. This does the trick. Jan turns off the computer, picks me up, and mooshes on me.

So far, our clowder is made up of local adoptees, but that was soon to change.

*

Tango, February-July, 2013. I'm the Cleveland Cat. Jan's widowed aunt adopted me from a lady bound for the rest home. For many years, Aunty and I, an adult, yellow short-hair of unknown age, were good company to each other.

When I began feeling lethargic and stuffed up, she took me to the vet. At first, he thought I just had a cold or an allergy. Then, he diagnosed me with diabetes and said I needed two shots a day! Aunty, not trusting herself to administer them with her shaky hands, tried to find me a new home where she could visit me, but had no luck. I kept going downhill and the vet said I wouldn't live much longer without insulin.

So Jan's sister, who lives near Aunty, bought some serum and learned how to shoot it beneath my shoulder skin. While she was giving me my morning shot, Jan began the seven-hour drive from southern Indiana to northern Ohio. That night, she watched her sister administer my next shot. The next day, after giving me my morning shot, Jan loaded me into her car and drove me nonstop to my new home.

I had no problem transitioning from an only child to one with siblings. I enjoyed napping on all the different furniture and excelled as a willing lap cat. My favorite activity was watching the feeders outside the master bedroom window: the Bird Channel on Cat TV.

My new vet and I experimented with the right brand and dosage of my insulin. We had no sooner settled on it, when a strange fleshy growth started to extend from one of my nostrils. It revealed the real cause of my sniffing – a tumor behind my right eye. The Js loved on me and enjoyed my company, keeping me as comfortable as they could, until I went to Heaven.

A youngster soon took my place.

*

Joey, 2014-present. Alone, as a tiny, yellow-and-white short-hair, I found my way to a horse barn. Different people came and went. Every time Jan visited her horse, she cooed at me. I finally gave her the honor of being the first human to pick me up.

I was really into tree climbing, then. Getting up was no problem, but coming down was terrifying. Once, I stayed in a tree in the pasture all night and the barn manager used a ladder to rescue me the next morning. That afternoon, when the Js came by. I showed off by climbing 40 feet up another tree. I got scared and began crying; they begged me to come down. I stepped wrong, fell a few yards, bounced off a limb, shrieked, and fell the rest of the way straight to the ground. The horrified Js assumed I was dead when I hit, but, quick as a wink, I rose and ran off – all my bones miraculously intact.

At the onset of below-freezing weather, after I survived the stomping of a horse who objected to my napping in his hay, the Js, tired of worrying about me, took me home. When my "equipment" descended, they realized I wasn't the Zoey I'd been originally dubbed, but, rather, a Joey.

Jan was over the top at living with a kitten. She called me lots of silly words – adorable, charming, cute, darling, delicious, luscious, precious, scrumptious, sweet, and yummy – I was afraid she wanted to eat me!

I'm still an active guy, albeit a bit on the clumsy side. I have razor-sharp claws and, like Calvin, enjoy distressing woodwork. I absolutely love windows, too – making curtain calls from the high, curtained, basement window sills and puppeting up from the low one behind the living room couch.

Jan calls me a "dog-cat" because I get along so well with the dogs, who tower over me (but not nearly as much as the horses did!) and come to her when she calls. Another of my monikers is "love bug" because I often curl up on her lap to purr, nap, and assume all sorts of yogic poses.

I also go by "milk fiend" because, no matter where I am in the house, whenever the refrigerator opens, I rush over for some 2%. I also enjoy drinking warm water from the rim of the tub whenever Jim or Jan bathes.

A young guy can only sleep for so long. When my battery is recharged, I dash around like mad and start playing "chew and claw" with the Js. For some reason, the party poopers yelp and send me away!

Like them, the next two cats to join our clowder were old fogies, too.

*

Arjuna, 2015-present. When I was wee and lost in a crop field alongside a road, a line of bicyclists rode by. I cried, but no one stopped. A lone cyclist appeared on the horizon after the pack passed. I resumed my wailing as the man came into earshot. He stopped, saying, "Little one, why are you here? It's getting ready to storm." Then he switched his jersey around so the wide, elastic pocket was in the front, and carefully tucked me inside. Curled up like a marsupial, I enjoyed a bike ride to his car and a car ride to his house.

I lived in the Js' garage for a few days while they tried to find me a forever home. Their friend Ed adopted me. He named me after the prince in the Bhagavad-Gita, a sacred Hindu text. I lived with him and his clowder for many happy years. When Ed died, the Js took me back.

Jim nicknamed me The Professor and The Black Smoke Prince due to my appearance. I wear a serious expression on my smooshed-in Persian face, and my fur is charcoal at the tip and white at the base. Jan simply dubbed me RJ.

I'm a quiet, easy-keeper who enjoys napping in soft places – sometimes in laps, sometimes in the open, and sometimes in secret hidey-holes.

*

Mindy Mae, 2015-2017. Another of Ed's cats, I accompanied Arjuna to the Js. A brindled short-hair built like a bulldog, I was also distinctive looking. My bowed front legs were too short for face scratching and grooming. The back half of my body was jacked up on long hind legs. My spine arced like an upside-down V below my ribs. And my insatiable appetite contributed to a belly that lowered my front carriage even further. Because of all this and my arthritis, I moved slowly and required a litter box with a cut out entrance.

While I first came to the Js, I was given the run of the house. At first, because Ed's house had been a one-story, the Js had to carry me down to the basement and back upstairs. It took me a while to build up my strength and coordination, but I finally mastered powering myself up and down those stairs, much to the Js' admiration. Eventually, however, I had so many accidents that I had to spend most of my time in the basement with a buddy or two.

I, too, was diagnosed with diabetes and required two shots of insulin a day. An abscess developed behind my left eye and drained from my eyeball. It cleared up after a few weeks of rinsing with a saline solution and the application of an ointment.

In spite of all my physical challenges, I was always happy. I loved my feline/human/canine family. I was always the first critter to approach every person who visited – friend or stranger – and wasn't afraid of anything, even the vacuum cleaner. My nickname? Sweet Pea.

One day my poor body finally gave out and I was welcomed into Heaven.

*

So, there you have it! We animals rest our case. We, especially the felines among us with our many wiles, are most assuredly the herders. And you easily manipulated humans, you are clearly the herdees.

Leader of the Pack
Brenda Drexler

"There's a new cat in town," announced Kitty Me with a long drawn out purr.

"Rrrr, who is he? Tell me all about him." Kitty Lulu sidled up to Kitty Me as if they were BFFs.

"Yes. Tell us," purred the rest of the she-pack.

"Okay. But ..." Kitty Me turned her back to the other cats, wrapped her full, silky tail around her, then looked over her shoulder. "... the first thing you need to know is, he's mine."

Claws scratched on walls and pavement. Green eyes narrowed. Kitty It flicked her tail back and forth. She moved gingerly past the others and closer to Kitty Me.

"Rrr," growled Kitty It. "What makes you so sure of yourself?"

"He kissed me."

A chorus of envious "Meows" echoed in the corner of the alley, near the dumpster of a high-class restaurant which they claimed as their turf.

"When? Where?" purred Kitty Lulu.

"Never mind all that," hissed Kitty It, as she pushed Kitty Lulu aside. "What makes this new cat something special?"

Kitty Me licked her paw and slowly rubbed it down the front of her long neck.

"He's so . . . feral."

This time the pack emitted a breathy gasp and a slew of whispers.

"Did she say feral?"

"Oh, my."

"Isn't that risky?"

"Whatever is she thinking?"

"She's not. You know how it is, Dearie."

"Purr."

"Where'd he come from, this feral cat?" hissed Kitty It.

"Does he travel alone or in a clowder?" asked Lulu as she moved closer to Kitty Me, purring affectionately.

"How did you meet this new cat?"

"Yeah, and why?"

"How did he kiss you?"

"Well, girls, if you gather round, I'll tell you how it went down."

Kitty Me perched on her throne, a wooden crate, where she was bathed in the glow of the streetlight. The light played on the many shades of silver and gray of her lustrous fur.

The she-pack moved in closer, eyes wide, expectant, hungry for more about the new cat in their midst.

Except for Kitty It. She stood her ground, twitching her beautiful orange tail. She listened, begrudgingly, as Kitty Me told about the sleek, handsome, blue-eyed feral that sported a black, glossy coat.

Kitty Me's claws came out, then disappeared into her fur as she lightly stroked her neck, briefly lost in the memory.

"I turned the corner at Big Jack's Fish Market, just out for a stroll, and there he was, surrounded by his clowder. They were sniffing around by the back door. You know how Big Jack keeps his alley clean.

"I was startled by the sight of them. He turned and stared at me. I couldn't move. My heart was pounding. Then he walked toward me, slowly and menacingly. His muscles rippled with every step."

A communal gasp again filled the air. Even Kitty It was spellbound.

"Oh my." Kitty Lulu's voice quivered. "Weren't you terrified?"

Kitty Me smiled at the girls. "He walked a circle around me, holding me with his gaze. And then he purred, in a deep throaty way, 'What's a beautiful feline like you doing alone on a starry night like this?'

"I couldn't speak. Something had my tongue. He circled so close that I felt his warm, fishy breath all over me. I promise, I couldn't help myself. I purred back."

"Oh!" The felines huddled even closer, whispering in hushed tones. "Then what happened?" asked Kitty Lulu.

"He circled me again, getting closer and closer, until the tips of his whiskers touched the tips of mine. I held my breath. I was terrified. Really, I was. My skin shuddered, deliciously.

"Then the door opened and Big Jack came out.

"'Get out of here, you bunch of trash pickers', he yelled at them.

"Cats were running in all directions, except *him*. And he said, "'I'll see ya later, Sweetheart.'"

"What's his name? You keep saying him."

"Let me finish. After they were all gone, Big Jack came over and petted my head. 'You okay, little kitty? You gotta watch out for those ruffians.' And then he fed me a piece of cod right out of his hands."

"You sure have old Jack wrapped around your paws, Girlfriend. Tsk, tsk." Kitty It turned to walk away, to do her own thing for a while.

"A girl's gotta do what a girl's gotta do," purred Kitty Me.

"Wait," a voice meowed, anxiously. "What about the rest of the story. You said that he …"

"Oh, yes," Kitty Me continued. "Right before he leaped into the darkness, he licked my face and slowly winked at me." She raised her paw and touched her face ever-so-gently between her brows. "I'm sure he'll be back."

Kitty Me stretched her body and purred softly. She

displayed her claws, briefly admiring them, and purred contentedly.

"He'll be back," she whispered to herself, then walked off into the darkness, swishing her tail, leaving the girls to envy her on their own.

Cat–A–Strophic Spelling
Ginny Fleming

Things might have gone much better if my ex-husband hadn't been such a dip and I wasn't such a bad speller. But he was and I was and, due to unforeseen circumstances, that day swiftly went to Hell in a hand-basket.

Nimrod was at my apartment – *again!* Dogging me. Whining and following close on my heels like a forlorn puppy. "Take me back, Barbie. I've changed. Really. I've changed!" Then, like the adult hyperactive child he was, he switched canoes in midstream. "Have ya seen my Spider-Man comics? I must'a left 'em here. You probably threw 'em out. *Right?*" Insert dramatic pout here. "You *always* throw out *my* stuff." Cue the midstream canoe. It spun back around for his impassioned ending: "Take me back. *I looove you!!!*"

Every – single – time Nimrod walked through my door (yeah, Nimmy's clueless and cruel parents *actually* named their only child that classical Victorian name; any wonder he preferred that everyone call him Nimmy?), every single time I was filled with equal parts confusing fondness, chuckling amazement, and angry disgust for this twit.

His dog-and-pony show might have been endearingly sweet if he'd not already taken this act on the road and bombed on Broadway. Nimrod's an actor, as is yours truly. Difference being, Nimmy could never hold a job, as he never stuck to the script, while I was a director's dream. I was known in the world of soap operas as the famed, phenomenally bad-ass character Peaches Kielbasa. That is, until the other day when

I died once again on *Promises To Keep*. This time they decided to kill Peaches off simply to bring in a teenage daughter she'd conceived during a nasty bout of amnesia – and birthed while in a coma – while, *known to no one else in the whole entire world*, she was held captive on a deserted island by that eccentric and quite madly-insane Scottish multi-billionaire Dingus J. Twiddle of the world-domination-seeking Twiddle Dynasty: I kid you not. Soaps. Gotta love em. Or change the channel.

It was kinda like a six-month paid vacation. I was scheduled solely for a few "flashback filming days." Hence, I'd recently found loads of time to rearrange my priorities. First priority: clean house. And when that bothersome task was finished? Ta-dah! Nimmy was out the door. But today? He was back and whining. I didn't have time for his crap. I'd decided the night before, this was Beauty Day for Barbie. I busied myself mixing up a huge batch of herbal hair rinse handed down from my Great-Great-Granny Rosaleigh Dupree. Granny Rosa, I called her. I had all the paraphernalia gathered, and her grimoire opened to her *special* recipe and other helpful chapters.

It was rumored Granny Rosa was a witch. Oh, not the kind who wears a pointy hat and flies on a broomstick, but a *real* witch. People spoke of her in riddles and whispers. Called her a "bad speller." What's the big deal about people who can't spell, you ask? Heh. I don't mean she couldn't spell *words*. I mean, some of the "spells" she cast were *bad*. Well, *mostly* bad. Legends said, she was kinda like the Wicked Witch of the West – only sweeter and prettier. But, Granny Rosa came from the Caribbean, which is east. Sigh. I'm babbling. Back to Nimrod.

That day, Nimmy's hanging around was just a little too much to take. He was especially obnoxious. I'd planned to devote the whole day to myself, but here he was in *my* apartment, dogging *me* about Spider-Man comics, for

Pete's sake. I'd finally settled him in front of the television with a PB&J and a tall glass of ice cold milk – anything to seal his mouth for a few moments.

I struggled to keep my mind on Granny Rosa's recipe and reciting the strange words she'd long ago scribbled in the old leather-bound book. Mixing the "eye of newt" (okay: sage and lavender) and the "pad of bird" (best I could come up with was a disgusting chicken foot from Schliemann's Deli) and all the other exotic ingredients the recipe called for. I stirred it gently and slowly, all the while murmuring the ancient spell's words. Just when I'd caught a faint flash of deep purple light "sparking" in the dark depths of the bowl, Nimmy piped up again.

"Barbie? Got any chips and salsa? Do ya, Babe? Do ya? Man! Sure could go for some salsa 'n' chips."

"Really?" I exploded. "I'm busy here. All you wanna yammer about is stuffin' yer face! Just *shut it*, Nimrod." I'd purposely called him Nimrod. He hated that name, but it never failed to get his attention. Nimmy looked hurt. To paraphrase Yoda: "Less I could care." I sent him a glare and a wordless snarling growl.

"Okay. Fine," he sighed, rather piteously. "It's clear to me I'm no longer the love of your life. I'll just sit here and starve."

"Moron. You huge hunk of wasted cells. It'd take you *months* to starve." I'd reached my rope's end. Suddenly, Nimmy leaped to his feet and lunged at the refrigerator. Detecting a disturbance in the Force and gallantly hoping to save me from the wicked, Darthly-wheezing appliance or searching for salsa? With Nimmy, reasoning was eternally up for grabs.

Time slowed, like it always does after one's suddenly fallen into "Insane & Idiotic Love" (IMHO, there's no other kind) or in the terrifying throes of one of my reoccurring running-from-zombies nightmares. Could Nimmy actually *know* where the refrigerator was? Could be. *Could* be.

More than likely, could be porcine pilots suddenly soared out of JFK as my weary brain pondered that appliance question.

My inner-dialogue of fruitless slow-mo tap-dancing ended in total horror as I witnessed my ex-husband's scrawny hip meet up with the bowl of spelled herbal hair rinse. Now, *slooow-mo* ruled the clock. Time stood still as I watched one of my favorite family-heirloom crockery bowls crash and shatter into a million shards. Magically charged sweet water splashed all over my beautiful cherry wood cabinets. I was utterly drenched and so was Nimmy. For what seemed eons I stood there quivering in mute disbelief, but finally I found my voice and shook the apartment walls with my outrage: *"Quit doggin' me around!!!"*

A wondrously billowing purple fog rose from the terrazzo tile and completely enveloped Nimmy. Just as it reached his chin, I saw true terror in the eyes of blue that first sparked my interest in my Broadway Bubba. My breath caught in my throat as I witnessed the big redheaded doofus collapse into himself. And suddenly, there before me, sat a rather goofy, but outrageously gorgeous, Irish Setter. I took immediate action. I fainted dead away.

*

After the world decided to visit me again, it felt warm and wet. Like something *icky* warm and *slobbering* wet. Opening one eye, I saw a distorted close up of a beautiful dog sitting in the same spot I'd last seen Nimrod. Licking my face. *Dog* was *licking* my face. A disgusting action I'd long ago banned from Nimmy's love moves.

Brightly gleaming reality dawned like the sun rising on a life-changing hangover. "Oh, (expletive that begins with 'S')! This can't be!" My mind was frantically making collect calls to the Otherside – *"Granny Rosa: HELP!!!"* But apparently she had her phone on silent/vibrate and the rest of the celestial universe wasn't cooperating one itty bit. It was officially weird. And there was a big goofy-assed dog licking my face.

Showing his concern, the dog asked: "Ru ro-kay, Rarwbee?"

Asked? The dog asked? That forced me into a sitting position, no matter I felt dizzy as a cat on a Tilt-A-Whirl. Covered in the slightly sticky but very nicely scented herbal water, I shoved my wet hair from my eyes and stared at the dog who grinned back at me – his tongue lolling to the side of his toothy mouth.

"What the Holy-F have I done now?" Holding my wet head in both hands, I moaned, rocking back and forth. Nimmy made to lick my face again. I recoiled in disgust, but then (out of shameful guilt?) surrendered and willingly raised my cheek to my ex. It wasn't one of my stellar moments.

Not surprisingly, what with having to scrounge up some of the hardest-to-find ingredients, it took most of the night to stir up a new batch of magic-spiced herbal water. Nimmy was absolutely no help. All he wanted to do was gnaw at a defrosted ham bone and try to get me to toss a tennis ball across the living room. But *anything* to keep him from barking. My lease didn't allow dogs, nor pets of any kind. So it was mix the magic water, toss ball, mix, feed dog, mix, go crazy, and mix until I was finally at the "stir and spell" part of the long night. Things seemed to be going well. Operative word: "*seemed.*"

I'd come to the last of Granny Rosa's tongue-twister incantation, taking care to enunciate the tricky words at the end: "Bellzoppon-Meandersol-Mempin-Hisszznick." (Were those last syllables a garbled *word* or more of a guttural burp? The instructions were very muddled). Just as I phonetically meandered my way through that meaningless sentence, coming to the climactic "hisszzing" part, Nimmy decided to test out a new modern dance act. He gracefully tossed the tennis ball into the air while simultaneously launching himself sideways from the sofa.

The ball zigged while Nimmy zagged. He landed on his side on the counter and another family treasure filled with magically enchanted herbal hair rinse became his unsuspecting victim. Just as the last of the long drawn out "hisszzzzz" left my lips, I was once more drowned in a deluge of spelled and spilled hair care product. I opened my mouth to bless my ex with expletives of undying love and surprised even myself with one long "*Meeeee*-ow." Flabbergasted, my first reaction was to slap a hand over my mouth, but I failed that. To my utter horror, I no longer *had* hands. Instead, the "fingers" I held before me were tucked compactly into pads of fur. Who has two thumbs and can spell like a witch? Not *this* girl. Le sigh....

The long night was a maze of blur. Perhaps if there'd been massive drinking involved, I could've made a teeny bit of sense of everything. But it's not every day one changes their ex into a dog and themselves into a cat. A decidedly *stunning* cat, but a freakin' cat, nonetheless. I was strangely transfixed when I gazed at my new self in the mirror. Due to some glitch in the cosmos, I'd transformed into a hybrid mixture of Siamese and Persian with a shining coat of ombré. Again with the purring "*Meeeee*-ow." Was I hot or what? But even though I gave myself high marks on the feline beauty scale, this pretty-kitty problem was an ultra-serious emergency. I'd have to find a way to get help with this lion-sized crisis. I found my phone.

With claws resembling alien Ginsu appendages, I managed to unlock my phone and click my way into "Chat," where I sent a badly spelled (*words* this time) message to Jana Pinato. My oldest friend in the world. If there was anyone who'd even come close to believing this nightmare, it'd be Pinato. Each tedious click of a claw helped me to slowly type out a message: "help pinato   plese hep   Nimmy an barbb cat dog   neeed youu   keey in under   door matt   coom now plese come now"

It wasn't long before I got her attention. And I wasn't a bit surprised by her response. My phone's ring tone, "Who Let The Dogs Out," was sadly apropos in these circumstances. I pawed the answer/speaker-phone button and Pinato's anger trilled over the miles.

"Cut the crap, Fahey." Her usual sweet salutation. "This isn't funny. Texting me in the middle of the night with *this* weak prank? You woke me from a sound sleep. You know that, Jerk? Drinkin' much? Whadda ya gotta say for yourself, Bitch?"

Eh…. "*Meeeeee-ow?*"

"That's right! Keep it up, Brainiac. You forget, I know where you live! I'll come kick your ass, don't think I won't!"

"*Meeeee-OW-ow-OWWW!*" I looked to Nimmy. He whined, covering his eyes with his paws. Great. Good goin', Mutt. Lotta help you are. I returned my attention to my phone. How could I get my friend to believe me? I started growling between meows. Three short meows – three long growls – three short meows. Any idiot would have recognized the Morse code signal for "SOS." It only took Pinato ten feline modified signals to decide something *might* be amiss. Even then, I heard disbelief in her voice.

"Fahey, swear to God, if this is another one of your crazy pranks. Are you trying to tell me you need help? *SOS?* Is *that* what's going on?"

"*Meeeee-OW-OW-OWWW!!*" Nimmy sweetly joined in on my desperate meow song, adding a woofed bass chorus accompaniment.

"Who's there with you? Why's that dog barking?"

Questions like that could derail us. It was a face/palm moment. I still had a face, but I lacked palms. Thankfully, Pinato had a flash of genius.

"Meow once for yes and twice for no, okay?"

"Meow."

"Yes?"

"*Meeeee*-ow."

"I'm confused. Was that once or twice?"

"Mee. Ow." *Jeez O'Pete.* That girl insisted on doing things *her* way. Always taking the difficult path. And, crap on a cracker, *that* has made all the difference.

"I'll take that for one meow. Okay, Fahey. Tell me what's wrong."

It was a dark and stormy night (okay: plenty dark, not so stormy) filled with meows and a few barks. Nimmy was either excited or he needed a walk. Luckily, I figured out it was the latter before he did his "duty" on the carpet. Getting the big lug to balance over the toilet seat was a circus of errors. But in the end, he proved to be a pro. Who'dda thunk it'd take my ex being turned into an Irish Setter to become house broken. And Pinato. Thank goodness for true friends.

About three hours later, between my meows (giving coded instructions telling her there was a key under the mat, and she was to let herself in without raising attention), Nimmy's whines, and Pinato breaking the "Secret Feline Code" in the first place, she was on a flight from her home in St. Augustine to New York. My bestie left her quiet and boring life shared with Terry "The Gray Man" Pinato, the nicest, but the most irritatingly *boring* man in the world, just for a 'paranormal pet rescue.' The Florida Cavalry was on its way. Nothing to do but curl up with my ex on the sofa and "purrrr" the big doofus to sleep.

*

The next morning, as the sun peeped through the window of my thirty-third floor apartment, Nimmy raised his head and yawned, just as the key turned in the lock. Pinato peeped around the open door and Nimmy loosed a howl of gratitude. I reached out and gave him a full-paw/four-claw slap on his snout. Amazingly, he shut his trap. Huh. Perhaps there's hope for the boy yet.

"Fa, Fa, *Fahey?* Zat *you?*" She stepped into the apartment and quietly shut the door. "*Nimmy?* Dude. What the hey-hey happened to you? *A dog?* You gotta be freakin' kidding me."

I balanced on my haunches, crossed my cat-arms and glared at my best friend (having practiced that trick all night). It took mere seconds for Pinato to understand the gravity of the situation. But it was a good two hours before I could meow the whole solution to our problem while she took notes. But with dogged determination (sorry, it was a *looong* night) and with a lot of gesturing, purring, growling, and meows I made it known to Pinato the monumental task before her. *She'd* have to mix the potion, while I did my best to guide her hands. *She'd* have to read and chant the incantation, while I pointed out the words by claw. Nimmy's only job was to stay outta the way. I truly doubted he was up for the task. Still, in all. We persevered.

Luckily, my labeled jars of herbs, spices, and "woodland findings" (gathered in Central Park by the light of the full moon) were mostly unscathed by Nimmy's goofy acrobatics, and still neatly lined up across my counter-top. We were running low on some very hard-to-find ingredients. But I remained hopeful we still had enough Jamaica Pepper, Garden Angel, Devil's Dung, Bat's Head Root, Dogtooth Violet, Goat's Pod, and the lesser magical herbs and spices to get us through. The mere thought of sending my friend out to my special store on a dark New York night made me shudder. My luck, she'd get locked away five to ten in Rikers for possessing spelled oregano.

I stared at the jar labeled "Graveyard Flowers." One

of the essential ingredients used in the majority of Granny Rosa's spells. It promotes persuasiveness and success in dealing with people, while attracting the notice of others – in a good way. I mainly needed it for its powers of boosting eloquence. Perhaps a concentrated hit of Graveyard Flowers would allow me to speak again. Perhaps if I could drop the "Jeopardy For Cats" game (I'll take "Meow-Meow-*Meeee*-ow" for $200, Alex) Nimmy and I could have a better shot at not wearing fur for the rest of our lives. Regaining the ability to speak ... words? Was it worth the risk? That jar looked mighty low. And by using it for speech alone, I'd be depleting the strength of the spell needed for changing back to our true selves. What to do, what to do. The clock was ticking. I heard "Final Jeopardy" music in my head. Imaginary sweat beads dotted my whiskers. Hmmm.

I shook my head, puzzling over this King Solomonish dilemma. Finally, pleased with my decision, I threw up my paws (though I'd not actually eaten them) and smiled to myself as best a cat can smile. "Let's do this thing," I silently told myself. "Let's put this puppy to bed!"

I turned my gaze back to Pinato and placed my claw on the spelling words laid out in the grimoire. Hopefully, for the last time.

*

The mixing of the magical hair care product went well. I believe Pinato must have actual witches in her bloodline – she proved to be a natural. So now, cat's eyes closed, I sat before her on the counter awaiting my anointing of Graveyard Flowers. She took the small vinegar oil bottle filled with spelled herb water and drizzled the fragrant liquid between my ears, allowing it to run in rivulets down into my whiskers, all the while speaking the (to her foreign) magical words. Perfect inflection, I might add. I dreaded opening my eyes just as I feared opening my mouth to test if this grand scheme had proved successful. I peeped out of my right eye and saw both Pinato and Nimmy gazing at me with such hopeful love in *their* eyes, all fear left me. I opened my mouth expecting to hear the dreaded "meow," but instead heard my regular voice snarl: "What're y'all doin' just standin' around? We gotta lotta work to do here!"

I had my human voice back. The rest of this crap should be cake! Knock on wood. Though I didn't even bother with that silly superstition. Can't knock with kitten-paws even if you wanted to. Next time you find yourself transformed into a cat, try it. Second thought, don't even waste your time.

Regaining my voice gave me hope Nimmy and I could and *would* regain our human forms. With my voiced guidance, Pinato made quick work of mixing and spelling the recovery potion. Nimmy was very good while we worked. (Good dog, Nimmy!) He seemed to be earnestly paying attention. I was so looking forward to seeing the big goofus as a *man*, I silently vowed to sit still for a cheek licking – *after* I reverted back and had an actual human cheek to lick. Problem was, our herbal stash was depleting. I doubted the power and strength of the magic-spelled mixture sitting on the counter before the three of us "hobbyist witches." It was crunch time. The proof would be in the biscuits, as Momma used to say. Pinato and I both turned our eyes to Nimmy.

He stood on his hind legs and placed both paws on the counter before me. I reached out and boop-kissed his doggy cheek. "Nimmy. You've always been a major pain in the ass, but I'd be lying if I said I don't miss your goofy face. Your goofy *human* face. Here's to seeing your ugly mug again." I looked in his puppy-soft eyes and added: "Love you, Bubba."

He whined, "Rahovve ru, Rarwbee."

"I know you do, big guy." I turned my attention back to Pinato. "Can't stand to see Nimmy like this. Let's do this thing, okay?"

She silently nodded and grabbed the squeeze bottle not quite filled to the brim with magical sweet water. The mundane dollar-store find contained the majority of our last ingredients. It was do or die. If this didn't work, it might never work. Perhaps Nimmy'd be a "forever dog" and I'd be a talking freaky-feline for the rest of my natural days. As she began the incantation, I closed my eyes tight, not wanting to witness the magical brew wet my ex-love's furry head.

Painfully long seconds passed. Finally, I heard Pinato's soft-spoken: "Damn." A single tear fell from my closed eye as real-world reality slammed savagely *hard* into my gut. We'd failed. No need to hope for miracles anymore. I was now certain Nimmy would forever remain a beautiful Irish Setter.

I opened my eyes, needlessly confirming to myself we'd lost the battle. Once again, Nimmy's tongue lagged out the side of his grinning mouth. As usual, he was clueless. At that moment, my heart *knew* I'd always and forever love Nimrod Fahey no matter what coat he wore. And I also knew there was only one answer that would solve our "bad spelled" dilemma.

"Pinato?" I asked. "How much potion's left?"

She frowned. "About a quarter cup. Not counting the last of your 'speech-brew.' But aren't they different spells?"

I sighed. "At this point, all that technical magic's probably moot. *Mix it together, Jana.* Just be ready to yell the words I whisper in your ear when you drench my head. Word for word and like you really, *really* mean it. Pretend you love me, 'kay?" I leaned in close and whispered the words in my best friend's ear.

I watched while she carefully combined the two containers into a full eight-ounce lavender squeeze bottle, and cautiously shook it and tipped it over my head. I barely had time to gaze into Nimmy's soft brown eyes and whisper: "I truly love you, Nimmy." Next thing I knew, my head's beautiful ombré fur was soaked and Pinato was yelling:

"QUIT DOGGIN' ME AROUND!!!"

*

More than six months have passed. The canine Faheys have a forever-home in St. Augustine with the Pinatos – Jana and "The Gray Man" (and their lovingly awaited future-critter). Nimmy and I have a blissful life. Romps on the beach. Midnight strolls under full moons. Enough chew bones to last a lifetime. Everything a pampered dog could want. And tonight on our moonlit beach romp, I believe it's time for me to whisper into the big doofus's floppy ears that we're expecting the pitter-patter of twelve, or perhaps more, tiny paws.

Life is good.

The Wistful Lion

J. Baumgartle

Lion hauls itself slowly upright
from the pride-scented grass.
Muscles strung with tendons
force distance from sleep
with a good stretch,
a tremor of shake.
The night is built into it.
The need for food orients its prowl
to a broad range of sounds and scents.
But hunger isn't as insistent
as it used to be.
The lion is strong, competent;
there will be game, and a chase.
The urgency is gone, though.
It eyes the darkening landscape,
registers the intricate details.
Growls softly,
that there isn't more to see.

Out of the Cabinet

Bonnie Abraham

Mistress Playit Wrenmother retied one of the many pink bows on her robe, pushed a blonde lock of hair off her forehead, and sat down in the first chair she came to. It had been a long morning. Her small covey of future mages had kept her busy as they practiced spells, asked all sorts of questions, and generally just needed her. They were a good lot, but they could be draining. Finally, she had given them a free hour before the midday meal so that she could just sit quietly for a little while.

To this day, she wasn't quite sure how the twelve students had become her personal charges, but they had unofficially "adopted" her and now called themselves Wrenmother's Wizards – WW for short. They took orders from no one, except at her request. Most of the time, that wasn't a problem. They had her standing order to obey the current Masters of the school. The problems occurred when other mages visited or were recruited to teach a special topic. Unless Playit had personally met and approved the new person, they didn't stand a chance. *I suppose it's normal after all we went through with Amurd*, she reasoned. *I should write a book about it – but no one would believe me.*

After musing over the antics of her charges for what, to her, seemed like only a few minutes, she realized almost an hour had passed. Smiling, she got to her feet and headed to her classroom where her wizards would be waiting to go to the midday meal.

The tables in the dining area all had school Masters

assigned to them for the sake of some semblance of order, and the students filled the seats according to available space next to friends, idols, or preferred Masters, but not at Mistress Playit's table. There were thirteen chairs and all were exclusively for Playit and her wizards.

Today, those thirteen chairs were empty and it was almost time for High Mage Cardim to enter. While the students shouted conversations at the top of their lungs, Master of Kitchens Sams paced nervously back and forth over the small patch of flooring in front of the doorway to the kitchens. What if the High Mage were to come in and see a whole empty table!

At exactly one minute before one o'clock, Playit entered, followed single file, like ducklings, by Lob, Nefron, Issim, Jareel, Thrum, Ves, Egal, Leal, Broka, Ona, Opak, and Ventula. Sams stopped and waited for Playit's group to seat themselves, then he bowed in her direction. "So kind of you to join us," he said, over the din of voices. "The High Mage is due any moment – Ah, High Mage."

Everyone stopped talking. The only sound was the scraping of chairs on the floor as all stood for High Mage Cardim the Red. "Be seated," he said. Over the renewed scraping of chairs, Playit heard him grumble, "I wish they wouldn't do that," as he passed her. He took his seat at his reserved table and nodded to Sams to begin serving.

With one clap of his hands, Sams triggered what he liked to call the Serving Magic. It was usually the only magic associated with the meals Sams prepared. All at once, the tables filled with platters and bowls of steaming meat-and-vegetable pies, gravies, breads, cheeses, and jams. The students cheered, grabbed for their favorite dishes, and resumed their conversations, shouting over each other with abandon.

In contrast, Playit's table was quiet. She looked at the

twelve solemn faces as they ate. "All right, who wants to tell me what's going on?"

No one spoke. No one even looked at her, but every fork stopped in mid-air.

Playit waited, knowing they wouldn't hold out long.

"Nothing," said Lob, finally. He was oldest – already Eighth Level, and the unofficial leader of Wrenmother's Wizards.

"Nothing?" said Playit. "When you are all so silent? Surely, you know I won't believe that."

Still no one looked at her. They were all very intently looking at their plates or each other.

"What have you done this time?" Playit asked.

Lob cleared his throat. "Well, ya see –"

"It wasn't our fault," said Nefron. His square face reddened and his already-porcupine hair seemed to bristle even more.

"Exactly *what* was not your fault?"

Ona and Ventula giggled. "The cats," they said in unison.

"They were cute cats," said Egal. His blue eyes flashed defiantly. "And they didn't hurt anything."

"We didn't conjure them," said Lob. "We just – sort of – let them loose."

"And they didn't hurt anything," repeated Egal.

"I see," said Playit, "and just where were these cats?" A picture of a stream of cats toppling over bottles in the Potions Room flashed through her mind.

"Well," said Lob, "they weren't really *anywhere* until they got let out."

"Perhaps you should start from the beginning." This was from Broka, always the rational one behind those owl-like glasses. She had once been painfully thin, but a steady diet of good food and love had changed her into quite a pretty little girl. *And so smart*, thought Playit, *already two levels ahead of her former classmates.*

"We were in our clubroom," said Issim. "Ona and Ventula were practicing some spells and –"

"It wasn't our fault," declared Ventula. "The door to that old cabinet just opened."

"Well, it *was* an Opening Spell," said Lob. "But it really wasn't their fault. How were they to know there would be something *in* that old thing? It's been there as long as we've used that room. What's it been now, three years?"

"Anyway," said Ona, "the cats came out – like, a whole bunch of them – and the room door was open – "

"– And they all just went out into the hall and were gone. We tried to find them," added Ventula.

"I take it, you didn't find them?" said Playit.

"Uh, well, not exactly," said Lob.

"We think some of them used Sams's old hidden entrance to escape," added Nefron.

"We didn't see any damage," insisted Egal.

"Exactly how many is a whole bunch?" asked Playit, ignoring for the moment the "not exactly" flag of warning.

"Twelve," came a chorus of voices.

"Who does the cabinet belong to?" Playit asked. The only answer to this was shrugs and head shakes. "Well, that's the first thing we have to find out." She sighed and took a long-overdue bite of the now-cold pie. She quickly chewed and swallowed the jelled mess, thankful that it was, at least, well seasoned. "And, Lob, what exactly *did* you find?"

"Uh, nothing." His face reddened and he shoved a huge bite of pie into his mouth.

"Right," said Playit.

*

The cabinet still stood open in the clubroom. Playit had seen it there many times but had never taken time to examine it. The open door revealed row upon row of drawers, the fronts of which were all carved into one large scene of a distant mountain, a stream, and a young man dressed in the long robes of a mage.

Playit recognized the young man, or thought she did – but the cabinet was far too old to actually be him. *Son of Murah, son of Bahana, son of Hana creator of Unsettled Waste, Destroyer of Malup the Renegade.* The familiar chanted lineage rang in her head. She closed the door and turned to her young followers. "You will need to go to Master Bahanamurah and tell him you accidentally opened his cabinet. Tell him about the cats and see what he has to say."

"It's Master Bam's, then?" said Lob. "Well, at least he's not likely to kill us."

"Will you go with us?" asked Ventula." Her already huge brown eyes were even wider with alarm. "We didn't mean any harm."

"Yes, I'll go with you."

*

On the way to see Master Bahanamurah, Playit and her charges met a very upset Master Bamau in the hallway. Playit felt a chill run up her back. The Master of Potional Wizardry!

"Good day, Mistress Playit. Oh, you can't imagine what has happened. I'm on my way to tell the High Mage." The usually dignified old man was waving his hands in agitation and his voice was an octave higher than normal.

"I'm so sorry for whatever it is," said Playit. "Can we help in any way?"

"No – no. I must deal with it. Someone has turned over all the jars of ingredients in the Potions Room. It mixes more with every breeze, and the school is very drafty, you know. Very dangerous – very dangerous. Excuse me, I must report to the High Mage." And off he went, robes flying, faster than Playit had ever known him to move.

"So, we know one place the cats have been," Playit said, just loud enough for the twelve students to hear.

*

Master Bahanamurah had only recently been added to the faculty as Master of Oral Magics, but he was no stranger to the school, or to the children who now entered his classroom. He had done twelve years of training there and had worked with Wrenmother's Wizards in helping to save the school from being taken over by a dark mage named Amurd. At that time, the young students had called themselves Wizards Against Amurd or WAA. They had disbanded when the school was safe and then "rebanded" immediately under their new name.

When he saw the group enter his classroom and noted their solemn faces, he stood and motioned them to sit, then came around and sat on the front corner of his desk. He made an impressive figure in his blue silk robe, his long golden hair braided and wrapped around his head like a crown. "This looks serious. How may I help you?" It was one of the things the students appreciated about Master Bam. He liked his jokes, but he took the students seriously.

"We have a confession to make," said Lob.

"Well, first," said Broka, "let's make sure he's who we need to talk to. Is the old cabinet in the WW's clubroom yours?"

"Yes. Is it in your way? I can have it moved, if you like," offered Master Bam.

"That's not it," said Lob. "Ya see, we – well, we accidentally opened it this morning."

"And some cats came out," said Ventula.

"We didn't hurt them," said Egal.

"But they got away," said Ona.

"And now," said Lob, " we just saw Master Bamau in the hall and he said someone had knocked over the jars of ingredients in the Potions Room and they were getting all mixed up – and we think it might have been the cats because we couldn't find them."

"You managed to open it?" said Master Bam. "Amazing. Which of you did it?"

Ona and Ventula raised their hands.

"Well, I must say," said Master Bam, "you are quite talented young wizards. Congratulations."

"But the cats?" said Ona.

"Yes, I suppose we should round them up before they do more mischief. Have none of you mastered any tracking or enticing magic? – Well, time to learn. Mistress Playit, I believe your cat's whiskers figure might help lure them in."

"I don't see how," said Playit, "but I will make one for you if you think it will help." She detached one of her pink bows, untied it, and knotted it into a loop. In seconds, she had gone through the steps to make cat's whiskers and automatically held the figure between her upper lip and her nose saying "meow."

"Perfect," said Master Bam – "only this time, let me do the sound effects." He grinned and, when Playit had completed the figure again, he sang "Meow" so invitingly that a large, grey cat stuck his head around the door and answered back.

Leal, who was closest to the door, reached down and lifted the cat into his arms. His blue eyes shone as the cat snuggled against him and began to purr. "I think he likes me."

"One down and eleven to go," said Master Bam. "Shall we try the Potions Room next?"

*

An hour later, they had been to seven different locations in the school, and eleven of the students carried recaptured grey cats. Along the way, all twelve students had mastered the cat's whiskers figure, but only Thrum was able to sing "Meow" convincingly enough to lure one of the cats. Thrum, everyone discovered, had a talent in Oral Magics.

"Well," said Master Bam, "that leaves just one cat missing. But, I fear I am at a loss as to where to try next."

"We haven't been to the kitchens," said Playit. She had tried to avoid thinking of the damage a cat might do in Sams' kitchens – or what damage Sams might do to the cat!

"I was hoping it wouldn't come to that," said Master Bam.

"Sams? – Kitchens? – Cats?" said someone. "Oh Creator, spare us."

Playit turned to see who was speaking. "High Mage. We didn't see you there."

"Bamau told me about the Potions Room, and here you are talking about cats. I presume there's a connection?"

"Probably. We've recovered all but one of the animals," said Master Bahanamurah. "But, that one may be visiting Master Sams."

"Well, I'm sure you can handle it," said High Mage Cardim. And he left them to plan their next rescue.

"If I didn't know better," said Master Bam to Playit, "I'd say the High Mage wanted nothing to do with an outraged Master Sams."

"Would *you*?" asked Playit.

*

The dining area was empty except for the tables and chairs. No sounds were coming from the kitchens. Playit and Master Bam tiptoed the last few steps to the doorway. The students waited back at the entrance to the dining area. They all loved Master Sams – but they knew better than to be around when he was upset.

Playit started to make the cat's whiskers figure, but Master Bam placed his hand on the string and shook his head.

Then he peeked around the door frame. He turned back around, put his hand over his mouth and doubled over, his face reddening. After a few seconds, he shooed Playit away as he snorted softly. When they were all outside the dining area, he gained enough control to explain. "He's asleep – with a cat curled up on his chest! He looks – quite content," he added with another snort of amusement.

When they had all moved farther away, they doubled over with uncontrolled laughter. Finally, someone sobered enough to ask, "What do we do now? Let him keep the cat?"

The question helped to restore order. "Well, I don't know if we can or not," said Master Bam. "I don't know all I should about these cats. Do they have to remain together? I don't know."

"What was their purpose?" asked Playit.

"They came out of The Waste with Hana. I think they had something to do with the creation of The Waste, but I don't know the whole story. My ancestors were big on recounting the whats but not the hows, if you know what I mean."

"So, if they were used in the making of The Waste, then separating them *might* undo The Waste." It was a grim thought. On the surface, it might have seemed, to most people, like a good thing to rid the land of such an expanse of desert. Most people thought nothing existed in The Waste but sand and rock. But Mages knew differently. The Waste was a great storehouse of magic – both the energy and the knowledge of. It was also home to thousands of magical creatures – the Rill, who looked like walking, talking rocks and grew to the size of mountains, and the transformed animals like their friend Pendy the mule who talked and worked his own form of Waste magic. Losing The Waste was unthinkable.

"Someone will have to explain to Sams. I'm sure once he understands the risk...." Master Bam's voice trailed off as he looked at Playit hopefully.

"Well, I'd rather it not be me," said Playit. "He's probably still upset with me for being almost late for the midday. And I think that's a bit too much to ask of the children."

"Goodness," said Master Bam, "we're acting as though Master Sams is a mean person. I've always found him to be reasonable – as long as I asked for snacks instead of trying to steal them. He does value honor."

"Good! Then it's settled; you will handle explaining to Master Sams. The rest of us will wait right here."

"You're as bad as the High Mage," growled Master Bam, but he went back into the dining area. Playit gathered up the children and explained that Master Bam was going to get the cat and explain to Master Sams why he couldn't keep it.

"Glad it's him and not me," said Lob.

＊

When Bahanamurah returned to the hallway several minutes later, the students were seated on the floor, leaning against the wall and practicing turning their loops of ribbon from whiskers to ladders, while the cats watched their fingers intently. Lob, who did not yet have a cat, looked up expectantly.

"The cat Master Sams has is not one of the twelve," explained Master Bam.

"Are you sure?" asked Playit.

"Yes. None of the twelve is a calico."

"Well, there were signs that the cats headed for Sams' entrance," said Lob. "Maybe one of them left the building."

"That wouldn't be good," groaned Master Bam. "That's a lot of territory to cover. It could be anywhere in the town."

"If I was a cat," said Leal, "I'd go to the fish monger's."

"If I *were* a cat," corrected Playit automatically.

"You know, that just might be where we should check next," said Master Bam, "but I don't think it's a good idea to take the other cats with us into the town. Let's take them back to their cabinet before we go looking for their companion."

*

The twelve students, eleven cats and two mages all trooped back to the WW clubroom and the cats were returned to the cupboard without incident. Bahanamurah began closing the cabinet door, then stopped. He leaned closer to the carving of his ancestor, studying it.

"What are you seeing?" asked Playit.

"It's Hana's robe. Look – around the hem."

There, along the hem, Playit saw the shapes of four whole cats, the head of a fifth, and the tail of a sixth. When she reached out and touched one, the cylinder with the cats moved forward, causing the tail of the one cat to disappear, and the body to appear on the other. "It's a dial." She took her hand away.

"Interesting," said Master Bam. "I didn't know that. But if I'm not mistaken...." He pushed one of the cats, causing the dial to move forward again. This time there was a click. "Yes. A hidden compartment." He slid the robe upward, revealing a small, dark compartment behind. Reaching in with two long fingers, he pulled out a tiny, leather-bound book. He held it close up and read aloud, "*Care and Maintenance of WasteKits.* – Well! That should be useful."

*

Now they stood in front of the fish monger's, but the stall was empty – no fish and no fish monger. "Odd," said Playit. "Graaber isn't the sort to just not come to work."

Master Bam went into the tented area to examine more closely. "No, if he hadn't come to work, the tent wouldn't be up and there wouldn't be any boxes for the fish." He stuck his hand into one of the boxes and said, "There are fish bones in here."

"But, surely one cat wouldn't have eaten *all* the fish!" said Nefron.

"This cat might have," said Master Bam. "Remember, it's been locked away for hundreds of years. And it's magic."

"You lookin' for Graaber?" called the merchant from the next stall. His tables displayed an array of fresh fruits, along with signs saying "DO NOT TOUCH." "He left about an hour ago. Must have sold out. I stepped away for a few minutes to get me a pastry down the way and when I got back he was gone. Not like him to leave his tent and stuff, though. There's another fish monger at the other end of the market if ya just have to have fish – my opinion's he's a little high on his prices, but...."

"Thank you," said Master Bam. "Let's go see. Along the way, keep your eyes on the look-out."

"Something's fishy about all this," giggled Ventula. Opak punched her arm, but he laughed, too.

"Shouldn't we try to lure it with your spell?" asked Playit.

"We would risk calling every cat in the city," said Master Bam, "but it may come to that."

"Perhaps," said Broka, "someone should have a look at that book you found, Master Bam. It might save time in the long run."

"She's right, you know," said Master Bam. "I had already forgotten about the book. Here, Broka. I have a feeling you can walk and read at the same time. Am I right?"

Broka grinned. "Yes, Sir. I do it all the time." She opened the little treasure and then, after only a second or two, gasped.

"It says not to feed them, Sir."

"Too late for that," said Master Bam. "What does it say to do if someone does feed them? And what are the consequences?"

Broka carefully turned a page. "Hmmm. It says they become guardian goyles. What are guardian goyles?"

Master Bam's face blanched. "They are servants of the four Guardians, who hold stewardship of all magic. Like the Rill, the goyles can make themselves look and feel like stone, and they are huge catlike creatures with very long, sharp teeth – and bad tempers. We aren't looking for a cat any more. Now we're looking for a huge, cat-like, living gargoyle."

"I think we found it," said Jareel.

"Where?" asked three or four voices at once.

"Over there." Jareel pointed across an open section of the market to a stall full of wooden and stone statues. In front of the stall, as though placed by the merchant for maximum attraction, was a granite-grey, six-foot cat-like gargoyle with ruby red eyes and two oversized incisors. And it was watching them.

"Does the book have any advice?" asked Master Bam.

Broka calmly pushed up her round glasses, turned another page and squinted at the small letters. "It says – hmm. It says, 'Once a waste-kit has eaten, its transformation cannot be reversed; however, with careful attention to a few details, the guardian goyle can be a useful friend. It must be assured that you are not an enemy of a Guardian or a Goldmaker. *See appendix for Goldmaker.*'" She began to flip pages toward the back of the tiny volume.

"Never mind the appendix. We know what a Goldmaker is."

"We do?" asked Ventula.

"We do," said Playit. "It would seem, this is up to me. I don't suppose this creature has a name, by any chance?"

"Oh, I'm sure it does," said Master Bam. "How one would *find out* its name is another matter."

"Ask it," said Broka.

"She really *is* a remarkable young wizard," said Master Bam.

Playit looked at him as though he had lost his mind. "Ask it?" she said. "Never mind. I know you aren't going to be any help." She turned, straightened her back, lifted her chin and walked across to the stall of statues like the Goldmaker she was. Only four Mages held the title, after all. *If I can't do this, I don't deserve the title.*

The goyle did not move, but Playit could feel its eyes following her progress. "I intend no harm," she said, forcing calm into her voice. "I am Playit Wrenmother, Goldmaker. May I ask your name?"

The goyle nodded its head – or at least Playit thought it did. The movement was slight. "You honor me with your name, Goldmaker. I am called Grraarr. What do you seek?"

"We seek you, actually – well, we were seeking your former self, the kit. I suppose now we seek information."

"What information do you seek?"

"We do not know all your history, only that you are, in some way, connected to the creation of The Waste. Does your being away from the other eleven kits endanger The Waste in any way?"

"They must be allowed to join me, now that I am free again. No harm will come to The Waste, as you call it, if we are allowed to rejoin."

"Will harm come to anyone – or anything else?"

"A wise question, Goldmaker. But the answer cannot be sworn, for it depends on too may things. We can only say that we will not harm what does not seek to harm us, the Guardians, or the Goldmakers. But we *will* guard."

"And we can ask no more. I will arrange for the release of the others."

Again, the goyle's head gave the slightest of nods, and then he closed his eyes.

Playit, realizing she had been dismissed, turned and walked back to the others. "Did you hear?" she asked.

"Yes," said Master Bam. "The idea of turning loose twelve guardian goyles on the city is a bit frightening, don't you think?"

"If they truly serve the Guardians, they will keep their word."

"So, how do we manage this? If one of them can clean out the fish monger, how are we going to feed eleven more?"

"You will ask Master Sams. He has a cat and he likes to prepare large meals."

Master Bam laughed. "Of course! But *you* will be the one to ask him. It's your turn."

"My turn! How is it my turn? You haven't fulfilled your task with him, yet."

"Someday, you will regret your treatment of me," said Master Bam, but he was already striding quickly back toward the school.

*

"You want me to cook for *cats*!" shouted Sams. "I am a master chef *and* Master of Kitchens! Cook for *cats*!"

"They are very special cats – from The Waste. And once they have eaten, they become guardian goyles," said Master Bahanamurah.

"Guardian goyles, schmoyles. What do I know of guardian goyles? They are just plain grey cats – not like my little Chessy who at least has pretty colors." Sams reached out to the cat sitting calmly on a chair at the little table and stroked her head.

"Perhaps you have something they can eat that doesn't have to be cooked? We just need to feed them and they haven't eaten in a very long time."

"Ah, they are *very* hungry, then?" He tickled Chessy under her chin. "Hungry," he said again, his voice softening. "Bring them here."

Master Bam was prepared. He stuck his head around the door of the kitchens and nodded to the eleven waiting young wizards, each with a cat in hand. "Bring them in."

Master Sams blew out an angry puff of air. "I see you were in no doubt that I would be a pushover."

"I was in no doubt that you are a good man, Master Sams," said Bahanamurah.

When all eleven students were in the kitchens, along with their cats, Master Sams, Chessy, and Master Bam, there was hardly room to turn around. "This is not working," shouted Master Sams. "Out! Everyone out! We will have to feed them in the dining area. I must have room to work. Out, I say!" The last was aimed at Master Bam who had tarried to see if he could be of assistance. "And do not let the cats on the tables!"

In the dining area, the students headed for their usual places, with Master Bam taking Playit's usual seat.

"Where is Mistress Playit, anyway?" asked Nefron, as he noticed an empty chair.

"She said she had something to take care of," said Issim, "but if you ask me, I think she just didn't want to be around when Master Sams heard what we wanted him to do."

"We didn't ask you," said Master Bam, though he had thought the same. "And as you see, all went well."

"And Lob's not here either," said Nefron.

This statement seemed to surprise almost everyone. "Now where did he get off to?" asked Master Bam.

"He didn't come back from the market," said Ventula. "I think that's what Mistress Playit had to see about."

Before anything more could be said about the missing boy, Master Sams appeared in the doorway of the kitchens. "I have prepared fish," he said. "I used magic, since I perceived that time is a factor. If you will line up your cats on the floor, I will serve them."

The students quickly lined up, each holding a cat. Master Sams appeared puzzled for a moment, then said, "Ah, yes. Plates, then cats. Very good." And he clapped his hands once. A plate of fish appeared in front of each student and they all bent to release their charges.

"Ouch," said Ventula. "It bit me." This was followed by similar cries from all of the young wizards as each cat bit his holder, then quickly licked the wound as though to apologize before beginning to eat.

"I wonder what that was about," said Broka as she rubbed her hand. "Look, it's almost healed."

The cats emptied their plates and sat, as though at attention. The changes were not all at once. First they appeared to be a little larger, and there was the hint of fangs showing below their upper lips. Their fur lost the blurry edge of softness. And they continued to grow – and grow.

Master Sams retreated to the kitchens where he cuddled his Chessy and promised to protect her. She did not seem concerned about the strange visitors.

"The transformation seems to be complete," said Master Bam.

"Now what?" asked Nefron.

The truth is, thought Master Bam, *I have no idea.* Thankfully, it was then that Playit and Lob arrived.

"I see everything is going according to plan," said Playit. The eleven goyles now stood, and faced her. "I am Playit Wrenmother, Goldmaker. Does one of you speak for all?"

"We are not complete," said the goyle in front of Egal. "Where is the one who completes?"

"The one – oh, you mean the twelfth, the one who calls himself Grraarr. He is in the village market. We are ready to take you to him whenever you want."

"Now," said the goyle.

*

They made a strange sight, even in Capital City where people were used to the strange sights generated by a school of mages and wizards. Eleven guardian goyles, paired with eleven young wizards, led by Mistress Playit, and followed by Master Bahanamurah and an uncharacteristically dejected Lob, made their way silently through the now-darkened and empty streets to the market and the stall where Grraarr waited.

"You have come," said Grraarr. "You will not regret your service to us."

"Where will you go?" asked Playit.

"Where we are called."

"Will we see you again?"

"You should not concern yourself, Goldmaker, with the paths of others. Your own path is marked by Creator. Seek and follow it. But these kits of yours – their paths are woven tightly with ours. Your path goes another way, and I cannot see if it crosses ours again. The kits will walk beside you for yet a while, but they are ours. We will come when they call and they will come when we call. They are Bonded."

"Does that mean me, too?" asked Lob, for while Mistress Playit had talked with Grraarr, the others had told him about the bites.

"Your path is woven with mine, but you are the Unbonded One. It must be so, for your safety. They must be Bonded for their safety. Their paths will remain woven. Ours must divide. So Creator has written in the stones. And all will be so and ever so."

Each goyle stood, gave a parting nod to Goldmaker and then, single file, walked silently away toward The Waste.

Ghost in the Machine
T. Lee Harris

Captain Miranda Morningstar's body jerked as she fell asleep. Not the optimal way to achieve the hibernation state, but it happened frequently if she was keyed up before entering the pod. Her Corps trainer explained it as a primal reaction where the brain couldn't distinguish between falling into the sleep state and a physical fall. Her Lakota shaman called it the snapping of the tether between body and spirit. On the whole, she preferred the shaman's explanation.

For Miranda, the initial effect of Ghost Walking was a philosophical mood. A feeling of oneness with the universe. She was one of the lucky ones. The sensation wasn't so pleasant for others. Some experienced fear or a sense of profound loss. For still others, the combination of biotech implants, hibernation pod and mental training required to become a United Americas Marine Corps Ghost Walker proved overwhelming. Some of them descended into a darkness, a debilitating paranoia that few returned from.

From her ethereal state, she regarded her own body encased in the translucent pod: tall and athletic, red-bronze skin and smooth black hair a testament to her Lakota Sioux heritage and, at that moment, so still she'd appear dead to a casual observer. The feeling was eerie every time – sort of like she'd walked over her own grave. United Americas' scientists never tired of trying to explain what the Ghost actually was. Their explanations always fell short. Neither could they explain why some people were more suited to Walking than others. Privately, Miranda found the struggle of science against spirituality amusing. To her, the explanation was simple. Her people had long understood that humans were dual beings of flesh and spirit.

Emergency klaxons screamed through the heavily shielded walls again, reminding her why she was Walking. Something big had struck the asteroid somewhere near Mining Facility 58-G and she didn't have time to waste contemplating the nature of spirit. She needed to get her desolid ass in gear. Her astral body shimmered as it passed through the bulkheads of the United Americas Marine Command Center into the stark landscape of the asteroid's surface.

Asteroid mining facilities were usually built well below ground since meteors and other space junk were a common hazard. Facility 58-G was built to that spec, using the host asteroid's pockmarked surface as armor and the bottom of an ancient crater as its main point of access. Only the UAMC command hub, with its sensor arrays and docking pads, had a presence above ground. In her short stint on the base, the outpost had taken – and survived – its share of impacts. That made the massive seismic shock from this strike worrisome. Even more worrisome was the sudden loss of all communication from that section of the facility. One big boom and everything went silent. Well, that was why she was there. To investigate where others couldn't. Ghost Walkers didn't need pressure suits – air or gravity, either, for that matter.

Phantom-like, she glided toward the impact site, sneaking glances at the awesome beauty arching above her. Space stretched endlessly. Distant stars gleamed and other asteroids in the belt threw back sunlight as if someone had strewn a double handful of tiny, misshapen moons across the blackness. Crystals in the dust beneath her transparent feet glittered like a carpet of tiny diamonds.

When she reached the crest of the crater rim, beauty was abruptly forgotten. At the bottom of the ancient depression was a huge jagged hole. At its center, the corridor that connected the outpost to the surface lay open to the sky, a metallic slash through the barren rock, point of impact marked by a starburst of debris. She was stunned. The sensors had indicated a large event, but in all her time with the Corps, she'd never seen anything like this. Not even in training vids. Whatever hit them had to be huge, but the sensor arrays were constantly scanning for incoming objects and nothing had been detected beforehand. Granted, detection *was* dicey in the middle of an asteroid belt. . . .

Summoning a mental map of the sprawling complex, she reviewed her best approach. Transport corridors were near the surface, but the outposts themselves lay much deeper. According to that rubric, the main structure would be under the hills formed by the rim of the ancient crater. The gash in the surface before her had to be one of the transport corridors. That might actually be a good thing. She approached the new-cut chasm with trepidation. Had the automatic defense systems kicked in to seal in the facility's atmosphere? A glimpse of a closed blast door a short way into the tunnel made her want to do a little thanksgiving dance. Too early for that, though. Instead, she skimmed over the blasted and twisted remains of the former passage and shimmered through the barrier.

The reinforced doors had shielded this stretch of the corridor from the worst of the impact, but massive ore transports and other vehicles lay tossed every which way like children's toys. Several still had their running lights on, beams shining crazily from their tumbled positions. Haphazard as it was, she was glad for it.

Ghost Walkers might not need air or gravity, but even she needed light to view the physical world. She glided through a spill of ore and stopped abruptly. A man in a shredded UAMC uniform sprawled on the floor, his body covered in lacerations. She didn't need physical touch to tell he was dead. The blood that pooled around him was starting to freeze and crystallize. Not good. That meant the environmental control systems were probably out. She hoped the outage was isolated to the impact zone. If the whole system was down, that would be bad news for any trapped personnel.

A little farther in, two more marines lay crumpled against a vehicle. She knew one of them: Captain Bridie Gordon. They'd come out to the outpost on the same frigate just a few months back. The other marines she knew by sight, but not by name. Anger flared, but she shoved it down. There wasn't time for anger or grief. Her job was to assess the situation, find out why these marines died and make sure it didn't happen to anyone else. Afterward, when it was finished, she'd take leave to go home and ask the shaman for a Sun Dance and the Keeping of the Soul to help their spirits pass into the next world.

Even in the dicey light, she could see that Captain Gordon and the other marine had the same injuries as the first man: burns and a cross-hatching of lacerations, some deep, some superficial. She frowned and looked closer. There was something odd about the wound patterns. She straightened and strode forward. Those details didn't matter at the moment. If the environmental control systems were off line for the entire facility, it was even more imperative to get inside and locate survivors. She kept insubstantial fingers crossed that at least one cradle in one of the UAMC security stations along the length of the roadway had been protected enough for a Carapace to survive intact. She'd need to merge with one before she could really be effective.

Light from overturned vehicles shone against another set of closed gates ahead. She made for them, but as she neared, something about the lower right corner looked strange. A trick of the light? No. There was a neat, perfectly round hole in the door about a hand span above floor level. It went all the way through. Astral lips formed a soundless whistle. These doors were composed of multi-layer military grade composites designed to withstand a direct hit from a plasma cannon. It would take an enormous amount of energy to burn through it. She glanced thoughtfully back at the fallen marines. *What the hell happened here?*

There were fewer overturned vehicles on the other side of the barrier and most of them were dark. Light in that section came mostly from government-issue glo-sticks scattered across the floor. The chemical light painted the corridor a stark blue-white. On that side, the area around the melted hole was scarred from energy weapon fire. More scorches streaked the walls and floor. She followed the marks until, at the far end of the hall, she found a smear of frozen blood cut off by another set of reinforced doors. Looked like someone closed it as they'd retreated. There were no bodies in evidence. There was, however, another melted hole.

The scene was repeated twice more before she located the first security pod. It seemed the defenders had been making for that goal, too. The scattering of light sticks showed all the weapons lockers open and empty. That didn't matter. That wasn't what she was looking for. She found *her* goal at the very back of the pod: a featureless door set into the wall. She passed through and stood in front of the dormant matte finish metallic form nestled in its contoured cradle at the back of the closet-sized chamber. She smiled. It was a Mark 7 Carapace. A stealth model. Not massively weaponed, but one of the newest currently available. Even better was the steady glow of green from the power indicators along the sides of the cradle. The Carapace had a full charge.

The Mark 7 was beautiful. The charcoal gray exterior was the usual androgynous humanoid form, but in the 7, the lines were graceful rather than robust as in the more heavily weaponed models. Dark, hairlike sensors on the head, spread mane-like over the shoulders and down the back, giving it an exotic look – almost like an ancient Kabuki wig. It was designed to disappear into shadows, move unnoticed and give the Walker within a 360 degree view of their surroundings. Given present circumstances, she couldn't have asked for a more perfect ride.

She flowed into the cybernetic shell, enjoying the tingle as she melded with the synthetic nervous system. After pausing a moment to adjust to the sudden flood of input from the unit's sensory array, she touched a palm to the door. It slid open and she stepped out into the room.

Obsidian optical sensors slid to the ID plate above the door before she initialized transmission. "Command, this is Captain Morningstar. I've reached Security Pod 206 in 58-G. I've merged with the Carapace from that station."

Major Sawyer's voice sounded in her head. His tone stayed official, but she thought she detected a tinge of relief in spite of it. "Glad you made it, Captain. Report?"

"Three known casualties, Sir. Captain Bridie Gordon and two members of her squad. Central causeway is destroyed at the point where it crosses under the ancient crater, but it appears the station itself is intact. Power is out, though, and the environmental systems are off line." After a moment she continued, "Sir, I don't think this was a meteor strike. There are signs of weapons fire and several sealed blast doors have been breached."

Alarm outweighed official in Sawyer's tone this time. "Breached? How?"

"Small hole burned through near the bottom. Fifteen, maybe twenty centimeters in diameter."

Sawyer was silent. When he spoke again, he sounded tired. "How do things look in the Security pod?"

Photoreceptors enhanced available light, allowing a better look than she had in her Ghost form. "More signs of a struggle in here, Sir, although less than in the corridors. Someone, probably the marines, have emptied all the storage lockers." Cybernetic fingers brushed the console. It was dark like everything else. "Security console is dead. I'm retrieving and reading the memory core." Fingers elongated and fitted into indentations on the console's side. A small click and the panel slid out. She withdrew a chip and inserted it into a slot in the Mark 7's forearm. There was nothing to download. "Chip's scrambled, Sir."

"That's not good. Continue recon and report any findings, Captain."

"Yes, Sir."

A beat later, he added, "Oh . . . Miranda? Watch your ass."

Her chuckle as translated by the Mark 7's vocal program sounded odd. "Yes, Sir. Will do."

The outpost was even more disturbingly cold and silent now she was experiencing it through the Carapace's sensors. Stealthing through the empty halls, she saw fewer and fewer signs of fighting the farther in she went. She also found no more closed hatches – which was a damned good thing from her point of view. The Mark 7 had the strength to force them, but doing so would be a noisy proposition, to say the least. The marine contingent appeared to have staged a strategic fall-back. At least she hoped that was what happened. The alternative didn't bear thinking about.

Before long, she dropped into a pattern: advance a few meters, pause, cycle through the Carapace's visual and auditory ranges, then advance a few more meters. Slow, but efficient. Even so, she almost missed the tiny sound of metal on metal down a side passage. Moving toward the noise, she cycled through the visual ranges until she got a hit. On-board computers locked in and enhanced the image. In the midst of a patch of energy weapon scorches, was a small construct resembling a Terran sea creature called the Brittle Star. Its six whip-like, metallic legs supported a globular body just about the right size to pass through the holes burned in the doors. It hunched over the twisted remains of another of its kind, apparently devouring it.

She stood rooted to the deck in horror. Miranda had never seen one in reality, but she recognized what she was looking at just the same. It was a Spiderling. The Emporium had arrived.

The Emporium was a loose consortium of beings who referred to themselves as merchants. They bragged that they'd sell anything to anyone with the credits to cover it. They touted that they would also procure anything a paying client wanted. The places they raided to fill those orders didn't usually use the word merchant, though. Those people tended to use terms more like pirate and marauder. The Emporium had rarely ventured into the Sol system before. Not because it was well defended, but simply because there was nothing there they wanted – until now, apparently. Miranda wondered what they were after.

Chilled, she retraced her steps to the main corridor, scanning to be sure there were no other Emporium units around, then switched to silent communication mode. "Command. We have a situation. I've just spotted an Emporium Spiderling."

There was a very long pause before Major Sawyer came back with a sharp, "You're sure?"

She locked onto the critter again. It was finishing the last of what looked to be its defunct companion's leg. Zooming in, she captured more images and transmitted them. "Yes, Sir. Dead certain. I wish I wasn't."

On the other side, the major swore softly. "Copy that. Continue recon, Captain, but run silent. Last thing we want is for them to know we're on to them. I'll line up some backup."

"Roger that. Morningstar out."

The Spiderling, still unaware of her presence, scuttled off. The UAMC didn't have a lot of intel on the Emporium, but one piece it did have was that Spiderlings were part of a larger construct. They also were known to assimilate the remains of other, damaged units so they could be rebuilt. This one might or might not be heading back to the main Spider. Regardless, her best bet was to follow it.

As appalling as the Emporium was by itself, Miranda found the Spiderling sinister on a primal level. She'd never liked spiders and, while these weren't real ones, they were close enough to awaken a deep unease. It was her grandmother's fault. Gran had been a good story teller and the often gruesome tales of Iktomi, the spider-trickster spirit were some of her favorites. Her tales had sent Miranda and the other grandchildren away with bad cases of the shivers – and the lessons of the stories etched into their minds.

Enough delay. She'd better get a move on before she lost her lock on the nasty thing. She'd taken one step forward, then the passageway filled with the shriek and flash of a plasma bolt. It hit the Spiderling from the side and she saw it smash into a hundred pieces before the effects of the plasma overwhelmed the Carapace's sensors. Over the echoes of the blast, she heard: "HAH! Gotcha, ya little roach-golem."

Input was returning to normal when a short, slightly overweight man with wildly curly hair, wearing low light goggles and a mining company uniform, darted out and bent to brush the smoking remains into a scoop. Glancing up, he caught sight of Miranda and froze. "Uh oh."

The man straightened slowly and took a cautious step backward. She was puzzled until she remembered the Carapace. Instantly, she held up both hands and said, "It's okay! I'm a friend! Captain Miranda Morningstar of the UAMC Ghost Walkers."

"A Ghost Walker?" The man stared for a moment, then wilted against the doorframe. "Whew. When I saw that robot form, I thought I was a goner." He straightened and held out his hand. "I'm Dr. Marvin Fleiss, mechanical engineer."

She grasped the extended hand out of force of habit. The little engineer shook it, then lifted her arm closer to his goggles. "Oooo! This is one of the new Mark 7s, isn't it? I heard we got some but I never got a chance to see one. Niiiice."

"Ummmm. . . ." She reclaimed her hand. "Thank you, Doctor."

"Marv."

"Doctor – Marv –" she amended before he could correct her. "I was sent to investigate what looked like a meteor strike on 58-G and seem to have found something completely different." She peered past him at his impromptu weapon. It was a plasma hammer like the ones the miners used to pulverize rock. It had been bolted to a tripod. Cables ran to a big battery strapped to a hand truck. "I'm a little surprised to find you here potting at Spiderlings by your lonesome."

"I'm surprised to find me here at all." He paused. "Waitaminit. You guys thought this was a *meteor strike?* No. No! It was the Emporium."

"I'm just figuring that out. How do you know?"

"Easy. I was in the middle of the first attack. I almost didn't get away. They invaded the main processing bay, closed off the transport tunnel then KA-POW!" As the engineer gestured widely, there was a tiny beep from his wrist computer. "Oops."

He tugged her into the room. Making a shushing motion, he knelt to mess with the cables leading off the battery. He whispered, "We schmoozed too long. We aren't very far from the processing bay . . . you better close your eyes – sensors – whatever . . . ." The hammer powered up as another Spiderling scuttled into the passage heading toward the remains of its comrade. Miranda barely had time to energize her internal shields before Marv cut loose with his makeshift weapon and the world became a blindingly bright place.

"HAH! Six!" he crowed. "I'll need to change tactics soon. Emporium Spiders aren't stupid, they'll get suspicious." Grabbing his scoop, he swept up the wreckage. Rooting through the pieces, he picked out a tiny disc that he tossed into the hallway. "Homing chip. They all have one. It can take a helluva lot of punishment – which is good – considering that one has now been blasted a total of seven times."

He dumped bits into a wall chute. There was a brief hum, then he grinned. "Trash recycler. I'm running it and the hammer off a battery from an ore transport. Those suckers hold a LOT of juice."

"Ummmm. I see. Marv, it would help to know exactly what happened. Tell me everything you can remember."

"Okay." He frowned, looked at his timer and nodded. "We're good, I think. It's been an average of two and a half minutes between Spiderlings. Like I said, I was there. In the main processing bay. The crusher there keeps breaking down. Ancient thing, probably built with stone tools, but there are times you just can't beat old technology, y'know? Anyway, the governor had gone out again, so I'd pulled off the side panel and was poking around inside it when people started yelling. I could see the loading area through the cooling grills and there was this big mechanical thing with six legs and a gazillion of the little guys swarming the room. It took me a couple seconds to realize they were the Emporium Spiders. I mean, why call them spiders when they only have six legs? Real spiders have—"

"Marv," she interrupted. "How many people were in the bay at that time? Was it just you and the other engineers?"

"Oh, no. Big room. People all over. There were five of us engineers, but a bunch more miners, techs, a few marines. Maybe twenty, all told. It happened fast. The bugs swarmed in then BOOOOM! Everything shook and the power went out. The security guys never even got a shot off."

"How did you get away?"

"I'd been working *inside* the machine so I guess they missed me and I wasn't about to wave: 'YOOHOO, me! Over here!' I got my back to the wall and inched out to the corridor. It was pitch dark, but I can find my way to this workshop blindfolded. There are always several sets of these goggles in the shop in case we have to work on something in the deep mines. Light is sorta bad down there. I figured they'd be useful now."

"Good thinking. Sounds like no one else got away, though – from that room, anyway. No telling how many people are scattered through the facility. Back at ground zero on the roadway, it looked like the marines put up a good fight, grabbed a bunch of weapons and fell back."

"Oh!" Fleiss said. "I think I saw them! A bunch of marines, anyway. They had what looked like most of the mine personnel with them. Tore past here a little while ago. Looked to be heading deeper into the mine. It'd be a pretty good idea. Lot of enviro suits, rations, emergency lights and stuff like that there. Easy to defend, too, I suppose."

"It would be." She looked around the workshop, then said, "You should have gone with them. It would have been safer."

"I thought about it, but then this huge wave of Spiderlings rolled through. The marines shot the hell out of them and kept running. You can't just squash one of those little bastards and be done with it, though. They rebuild themselves. I knew there'd be more."

"So, you cleaned up the mess, recycled it, tossed a homing chip out and waited with your plasma hammer."

"Yeah. Pretty much."

Miranda was glad the Carapace wasn't capable of facial expression. If she'd been in her flesh and blood body, no amount of training could have kept a smile from her face or contained a peal of laughter. She was quiet a little too long.

"What?"

"Nothing, Marv. Nothing at all. I was just savoring the beauty of it."

"So, what do we do now?"

A tiny scrape just outside snapped her head around. Six Spiderlings were crawling across the wall. "We change tactics. They found us."

Training took over and she spun into motion. Cybernetic legs lofted her into the hall, a graceful turn in mid-leap brought her shoulders flat against the far wall. Her aim was perfect and she smacked squarely into three of them. They gave a satisfying squee-crunch and fell to the floor, useless.

The remaining three tried to fan out. She swatted one from its perch with such force, it cracked against the opposite wall, snapping off two legs and crumpling the rest. Miranda brought her foot solidly down onto it as she pivoted a kick toward its companion. It lashed out with its tentacles, making shallow furrows in the Carapace's surface. The sixth dropped onto her left shoulder and dug in. Its companion did the same on her right calf. Together they pumped electricity into her. It tingled along the Mark 7's artificial nervous pathways and she suddenly knew the cause of the three marines' deaths. If she'd been flesh-and-blood, she'd have been jerking in fatal spasms – and they were cranking up the power. She wasn't about to let them find the right amount to take out a Carapace. Pivoting, she smashed her shoulder into the workshop's metal doorframe. The Spiderling crunched and dropped off. The last one tried to release and run for it, but she scooped it up, smashed it against the wall and crouched, opening all senses for other enemies in the darkness.

"Wow! Just wow!" Dr. Fleiss ran fingers through his wild curls. "That was beautiful! Like a dance."

The vocal program translated her chuckle better this time. "Now, I think we take the fight to them. Can you lead me to the processing area?"

*

Captain Morningstar wasn't sure what she expected to see when she entered the main processing bay, but the pristine, neat-as-a-pin scene she found wasn't it. The place looked as if nothing had happened. That is, if you didn't count a dozen Spiderlings stacking semi-translucent cylinders, each with a humanoid form suspended in it, at the far end near the loading bays. Marv's guestimate was on the money – she counted nineteen cylinders. A larger Spider, perhaps four feet at its tallest point, was supervising the activity.

It appeared the Emporium was there for people.

If Miranda's inner child found the Spiderlings unnerving, the bigger Spider was downright terrifying. *Thanks, Gran.* Standing taller, she strode toward the larger construct and called, "You've invaded United Americas territory, Spider. Stand away from the captives."

The thing pivoted to face her, although she'd have been hard pressed to identify front from back any other way. "Ah!" it said in an oddly accented voice. She wondered if it was using a translator. "They've sent us a Ghost Walker. I wonder how much you'll fetch on the open market? A Ghost Walker has never been up for auction before."

Once again, Miranda was grateful the Carapace didn't allow for facial expression. If the Emporium attempted to capture a Ghost Walker, all they'd wind up with was a very expensive – but empty – Carapace. Apparently, the Emporium's intel on the UAMC was no more complete than the UAMC's was on them.

Good bluff, Iktomi, but you blinked. Aloud, she said, "Stand away from the captives."

"I think not." At a shrug-like gesture, the remaining Spiderlings melted into the main Spider. It grew visibly larger with each addition. "These mining engineers have been paid for. There are fewer than hoped, yes, but the other humans will make up for the loss."

"Our people are not for sale."

"*Everything* is for sale, little Walker." The Spider moved slightly closer. Miranda let it.

"Stand away from the captives," she repeated.

"Or what?"

She launched into an aerial somersault that closed the distance between them and brought both feet down on the Spider's front end. The impact smashed it to the floor. Miranda used the recoil to flip backward and land several feet beyond her starting point.

The voice was still the eerily calm, synthesized one that was at odds with the jerky, violent movement of the construct. "I do not break as easily as my smaller counterparts, Walker. Are you surprised?"

It lashed out with a tentacle and wrapped it around her, lifting her from the floor. Electricity flowed. Sparks arced and danced across the Carapace as she dug cybernetic fingers into the constricting arm and ripped. The appendage broke with a deafening crack and she dropped to the floor, scrambling farther away. To her horror, the severed tentacle heaved and dissolved into Spiderlings that swarmed back to the main Spider to recreate the limb.

"I do not have the equivalent of your human laugh in my databanks, Walker, but you see you cannot win."

It lashed out again. Miranda dodged and somersaulted past the huge rollers of the broken-down crusher. *Closer. Iktomi, a little closer. I'm glad I heard Grandmother's stories. It pays to remember the lessons of the spider-spirit on using one's wits to overcome a larger enemy.* Even as she regained her feet, the Spider lunged. She evaded, but the tip of one tentacle grazed her side, knocking her down and slicing deeply into the Carapace. She let momentum carry her well out of range, then called, "NOW, MARV!"

The room strobed with the pulse of plasma as Dr. Fleiss unleashed the full power of the hammer.

The Spider crashed and skidded along the floor, one leg buckling as energies ripped a gash along the featureless body. It thrashed against the decking, trying to regain footing. A second burst severed another leg. The construct turned with the blow and skidded, bringing itself closer to the hammer. One flailing tentacle caught the tripod, sending both weapon and engineer flying. Marv struck the side of the crusher with a dull thud. He slid to the floor, the hammer rocking inches from his motionless fingers.

She tore her gaze from the still form with difficulty and turned back to the Spider. She wished she hadn't. The monstrous body rippled, damage healing before Miranda's horrified eyes as if it never happened. Anger surged inside her. This time, she let it happen. Fury propelled her as she flung herself forward, grabbing the closest leg and jerking the Spider farther away from the fallen engineer. A dive and roll brought her within reach of the hammer. Snatching it up, she wrenched the mangled tripod off, then leveled it at the near-healed Spider.

"I told you before. Our people are not for sale." She pulled the trigger.

The plasma hammer wasn't designed to be used as a hand-held weapon and it took all of the Carapace's strength to hold it and herself steady as it heaved and bucked in her arms. Its roar filled her mind like a war chant of pure energy. The construct exploded. Tentacles crumpled before the assault. Spiderlings that tried to crawl away were shattered and their remains were smashed again until there was nothing left to fire at.

Slowly, she lowered the weapon and leaned back against the solid bulk of the crusher, letting the backwash of the surge pass. There was no physical adrenaline rush for a Ghost Walker, but the aftermath of extreme emotion left her shaky and drained, nonetheless.

Dr. Fleiss groaned and sat up. "Gevalt. That was a light show and a half."

Miranda knelt beside him. "Are you okay?"

"Okay, I'm not sure about, but I gotta be alive. Dead wouldn't hurt so much." He ran shaking hands over his face and asked, "What happened?"

"I think we won." She gave his shoulder a companionable squeeze. "Now, let's get this junk into the recycler before it can reassemble itself and see about getting our people out of those pods."

Covenant Restored
Glenda Mills

The alarm on her phone went off at 8:00 A.M. Rita rolled over and silenced it. She saw the little thought bubble in the upper left corner and opened the message. It was Jeremy asking her to meet him for lunch. He'd sent it at 6:30 A.M. Of course he had. She was still getting used to a friendly morning person. Steve, her ex-husband, had been a morning person, too, but he'd always called her lazy because she liked to sleep in when she could. Jeremy's only concern was that she got the sleep she needed. Her eyes moved up the screen to the text from the night before.

"Steve hated cats because they were too independent. He liked dogs because he could be mean to them, and they would always stay loyal to him and come back in hopes that he would love them. Sounds like the same way he treated me, huh? I guess I wasn't much smarter than the dogs. Gee, that's a gloomy thought. Guess I was just another bitch in his kennel."

Rita winced. Note to self. No more late-night texting, especially in the mood she had been in last night. Jeremy had simply responded, "I don't know what to say to that."

Jeremy was more than a friend, at least in her heart. He hadn't really made anything official, yet, and her level of anxiety was rising steadily. They had been friends for years. Shortly after the divorce was final, she had seen him at a Bible study they both attended. One question led to another, and soon they were meeting for coffee. Jeremy had a lot of ideas for projects – books, Bible studies, and a foundation he wanted to start. One project became two, then three, then more. They met often. The discussions became increasingly personal. They would get together for dinner or share a bottle of wine. Her emotions had gone where she never meant them to go. Inevitably, the night came when she was at his house, and it got really late. It wasn't prudent for her to drive home as tired as she was, so she slept on his couch. The next time it happened, she slept in his bed, and so did he. Years of anger and resentment had melted away at the gentleness of his touch. A passion was awakened in her that she hadn't known still existed, and she gave herself over to it, without guilt or reservation.

She heard three beeps from downstairs: the coffee was ready. She wrapped a robe around her Eeyore nightgown and made her way to the kitchen. She poured a cup, complete with sweet Italian cream, and sat down at the kitchen table. A stack of papers glared up at her.

"Yeah, I know. I need to get you filled out. I'm working on it, okay?"

Procrastination was just one of the many gifts Rita possessed, and, when the task at hand was filling out thirty-seven questions about her marriage in the hopes of getting an annulment, it was easy to put it off. She needed the paperwork to go through, especially now that Jeremy was in the picture. She had answered the first twenty-three questions; only fourteen more to go. Question twenty-four wanted to know about her former spouse's family and childhood. It had nine parts.

One thing was becoming crystal clear: her marriage had been a train wreck waiting to happen from the beginning. Still, this was not what she had planned thirty years ago, when she vowed to stay with Steve for life. She found herself in a relationship limbo, civilly divorced and yet married in the eyes of her Church.

118

"How did I end up here?" she said out loud. It wasn't the first time she had asked herself this question. She knew the why's of the divorce. Steve was on mistress number four by the time she left. He had stopped giving her any financial support to raise their youngest son, the only one still at home. He was mean and hurtful every chance he got. She knew why she had left. What she couldn't wrap her mind around was the realization that she now hated someone who at one time she had loved with all her heart, someone she had had four children with, someone who had been there for the best and worst of almost thirty years of her life.

Her coffee cup half empty, she went upstairs to get dressed for the day. She thought back to her text message last night – to the hurt that had spilled out in words. She'd never really thought too much about the whole cat/dog mentality. Growing up, she'd had both and loved them equally. It wasn't until she'd met Steve that she'd realized there were people who were one or the other.

She opened the upstairs closet and sighed. It was still full of boxes from the move. It had been a surreal experience to pick apart her life one piece at a time, to untangle all the memories. Some things were easier than others, of course. She knew the elf Christmas tree ornament and the stocking with Steve's name on it stayed. So did the Nativity set that had been reverently placed under the freshly cut tree every year from their first Christmas to their last. Before that, it had been Steve's. She left his grandmother's rosary, even though he'd given it to her when she joined the Church shortly before their wedding. Somehow, it seemed like the right thing to do. She tried to remember who had given them each item as she picked it up. Did his aunt give us that dish for a wedding gift? Where did the vase on the table come from? And, with each decision, Rita came one step closer to walking away for good.

She had taken all the wedding items, including the pictures, her bouquet, and the bride and groom teddy bears that had sat on top of their cake. Steve had made it obvious that he didn't want any of them. Rita couldn't bear to throw them away. One item that had not gone into the box was her wedding ring. She'd never stopped wearing it, in part as a reminder that, in the eyes of the Church, she was still married. But there was more to it than that. She wasn't sure exactly what the more was, but the idea of taking it off was unsettling at best, a fact she had recently found out the hard way.

She turned the ring a time or two, noticing how it shone in the morning sunlight coming through the bedroom window, too bright for its thirty years. Years ago, she'd had her wedding ring and engagement ring fused together in the back, so they were one. Rita had started her new job at a daycare facility two months before, a job which required her to wash her hands many, many times each day. One day, as she was rinsing her hands, she saw something flash in the sink. She didn't think too much about it at the time, but when one of her coworkers asked her where the diamond out of her engagement ring was, she realized what had happened. As she looked down at the mutilated prong and the missing stone, she knew where her diamond was. Her boss had not offered to pay the plumber to come out and check the trap in the sink, and Rita didn't feel like she could request he do so. That night, she had prayed to God for a miracle. If there was any way possible, she wanted her diamond back.

One day the following week, Rita had looked up just in time to see plumbers leaving the building. Before she could catch them, they were gone. She couldn't believe it. But, shortly after they left, the toilet that they had been called to fix refused to shut off. Rita's boss called them back. This time, she was ready. When they finished the job they were working on, Rita asked them to check the trap in the sink for her diamond. When the water spilled out on the floor, her diamond was there. She'd had it repaired the next day.

Rita had told her spiritual director about losing and then finding her diamond. As they talked, she explained how ridiculous she felt about the emotional attachment she had to this ring. Jeremy had sold his. Her sister had sold hers. Why was it so important to Rita to have it?

Father Eric had leaned in closer and said, "When you were married, your covenant was between you, Steve, and God. By bringing the ring back to you, God is letting you know that, even though you and Steve are not still together, God's covenant with you has been restored. He loves you." She had felt the tears welling up. Ever since the divorce, she had felt sure that God was, at the very least, disappointed with her. It was so easy for her to doubt His love, especially when she couldn't find it in her heart to love herself.

She turned the ring once more. "Thank You, Father God." Rita glanced at the clock on her bedside table. It was almost 10:00. "You're a mess," she said, as she pulled out a pair of jeans and a University of Kentucky sweatshirt. The boxes offered no opinion either way. She realized she hadn't responded to Jeremy's text inviting her to lunch, yet. As she scrolled down to answer him, she saw again the text from last night. Steve hated cats. He also hated her. Everything was upside down and sideways. She was in a place she never wanted to be, trying to navigate a life she never asked for. But she had Jeremy, at least for now, and she had God, now and forever. All the other craziness would come together, somehow. Until then, there was one more thing she needed to do. She texted Jeremy back and told him she would be coming over soon, but first she had to make a stop at the animal shelter and see about adopting a cat. She hoped he wouldn't mind, but reminded herself quickly that, if he did, he'd just have to get over it.

Courting Mel
Brett Alan Sanders

For Anita

On the afternoon of her surprise fortieth-birthday party, Mel showed up at the print shop where she had lovingly struggled (for some twenty hours per week during most of the last fifteen years) over the graphic designs of old-style children's books with their ornate calligraphy. This newest one was called *Person the Cat and the Mississippi Mule*, text by retired high-school English teacher and librarian Margaret Meadors and art by herself, Melanie Gottlieb. The shop was a picturesque building of hand-hewn pine logs, thoroughly groomed and decorated, in a row of similarly picturesque buildings in her hilly Hoosier town's scenic old business district. Tourists and sightseers would flock to the area in droves during the autumn season when the trees were most magnificently colored and the scents of hot apple cider and chocolate fudge no less seductive.

It was spring, now, a Saturday in May after the twin national crises of terrorist attack at home and foreign incursion into Afghanistan. The streets were quiet but still alive. She was alone at her work table (having come in by herself to catch up some loose ends) when Cameron pulled up to the curb and honked his horn.

Cameron had invited her out for an elegant evening instead of the usual board games at home or stroll through vale or woods, or the rare movie or the more common fast food or window shopping in town. But her mind was not on romance. It had not been for some time. This blue funk had been settling in on her for quite a while, perhaps through a pair of dreary winters, imperceptibly at first but growing more pronounced with the deepening of recent tensions with one child and of this more broadly threatening Armageddon.

"Penny for your thoughts," Cameron said, observing her sullenness with some alarm.

Mel just sighed and looked away, staring distractedly out the passenger window. A moment later she sighed again.

"Look. I don't know what to couch this in, so I'll just be direct. The world as we've known it is in collapse, the God of comforts strangely absent, and I'm not sure I love you anymore. That's it, I'm finally out with it! And on the third point, I'm thinking maybe we should take a break for a while. Or maybe just call it quits."

Cameron, after all his renewed efforts to please her, thought she was being rather petulant, though he did share her uneasiness about the fragile state of the cosmos. He glanced at her from where he sat behind his old Love Bug's wheel, the ancient yellow Volkswagen Beetle he chugged to school in every weekday morning at a neighboring county's alternative high school. He raised his brows, tilted his head to the right. Otherwise, his characteristically bemused stone face did not change much.

"Oh, really? Big words for the sweet little hippie girl I thought I married."

"You think it's funny. I'm not joking."

"Didn't say you were. Don't mean to imply it."

She opened the glove compartment, fiddled around for some tissues, began dabbing at her eyes.

"It's not to get back at you, if that's what you think."

"*Tell* me what to think. I'm drawing a blank on this one."

She sighed. He turned left through the rich foliage into the state park.

"And there's no one else, either."

"I'd have never thought that of you."

"What would be the point of it, anyway? I'm too depressed to keep things together with you and the kids. And, anyway, it's been like herding cats all these years, or alien creatures from outer space. It's a wonder I didn't wig out on you long ago. How could I possibly manage with a lover on the side?"

She laughed and rolled her eyes, startled by the readiness and the spiteful self-concern of the initial confession. And by how these last words came crashing after it, too, like one more stretch of raging mountain rapids. She looked down at the floor through this lull in their lovers' quarrel, dabbed some more at her eyes while he pulled up to the ranger's greeting station and paid the entrance fee. Then she went on.

"And it's nothing you've done. You've been good enough, I suppose."

She started sobbing. Cameron, forcing himself to swallow his own rising sorrow, patted her knee with his free hand. He lifted it to shift gears. He set it down again.

"Oh, I don't even know what all it is, tired and disillusioned, maybe, but I just don't think I can do this anymore. I don't know what to do or what it is I want. But I'm pretty sure it's not you. Not you who can help me out of this, anyway. *Whatever* this is."

Cameron, in a desperate maneuver to lighten the mood, switched up his vocal stylings.

"So it's neither I m'love blames nor I she wants."

"Sorry."

"What can I say, m'love? Naturally, I'm grieved. Won't ye favor me with a'nuther chance?"

"Oh, stop it, already! Stop trying to be nice when you should be shouting at me. I'd deserve it if you shouted.

This would be so much easier if you'd just start shouting. And enough with the dopey accent!"

But the boyish sound of that cadence recalled to her the precise moment she had first laid eyes on him more than twenty years earlier, earnest-looking blond with an extra-cheese-and-mushroom pizza delivered to her dorm room. When Mel opened the door and saw him, she took in her breath and giggled. Cameron bowed and put on his best brogue, which, despite a year in Ireland and like other voices he would try on as the mood hit him, was not entirely convincing. At the memory, she fumbled for more tissues, lurching between hysteria and a complementary urge to kiss him.

"Nothing personal, Cameron. None of it's your fault, I know it's wrong of me to feel this way. I don't mean to hurt you. Anyway, you wanted to know what I was thinking."

"Oh, I'm so sorry, Melanie Gottlieb, but that answer is not—"

His voice cracked with the unmanly tremor of a choirboy's falsetto. He pulled himself together, drew his chest in with a slightly musty breath, and swept forward with the actor's practiced flair – behind weathered teacher's mask, performer on life's lowly stage – before the piercing barbs of a crew of seasoned mockers.

"– correct. Thank you for playing, anyway. And stay tuned for more of south-central Indiana's favorite game show, *Dollars and Cents for Cerebrations*."

*

When they walked into the inn, Mel was startled to see what, if not her own wild-child Zoë's face peeking around the open door of the banquet room and then ducking back in, had to be her incarnate shadow's; with, if Mel was not mistaken, the same general pattern of facial piercings. Then, as Cameron guided her through those doors, a full month ahead of her actual birthday, she saw the black balloons and banners everywhere and all those familiar faces. At the front of them was plump and pretty Zoë, with psychedelic pink hair like Ozzy Osbourne's kick-ass daughter Kelly. She also had a ring in her lower lip, another in each nostril and over each eyebrow, and one more in her tongue. Zoë stuck out the latter at her longsuffering mother as she opened her mouth to screech, in her best metal-head voice: "Surprise!" She raised one arm in her biker-girl-from-Hell salute and flashed the latest of the colorful tattoos she had recently acquired.

She had gotten them from her biker gang-leader boyfriend Mongo's tattoo parlor where no one demanded a parental permission. Her parents, afraid of her running off to some godforsaken desert with this wild-bearded hulk of a twenty-eight-year-old man (to her seventeen years), never to be seen by them again, had not pressed charges for those violations or for the Lord-knew-how-many statutory rapes. The first tattoo she had gotten, which she brought home unannounced one day along with this first lover, was on her tender bottom: a black and orange Monarch butterfly. She actually unfastened her frayed denim shorts and turned her back to her mom and displayed it: her patient and obedient Mormon mom who had married, then borne and raised children, baked bread, all of that and then some for all these years just as the prophets commanded: those gentle, solemn old men who would also remind her that this rebel daughter's body, like her own, was a temple of the living God; and of a parent's "awesome responsibility" to keep her children from Satan's many and insidious snares, including the birth control pills and condoms she was guiltily supplying this precious baby with.

Mongo came from behind Zoë and planted a wet one on Mel's cheek. From the smell of things, he had already been drinking, but his hair was slicked back and Zoë's impish smile told Mel they would be on their best behavior. Then, except for the eldest who was far from home, came the rest of the five children with all those obligatory hugs and kisses. Her good friends from the shop, who had never given the slightest hint of any conspiracy, beckoned from a nearby table for Mel to take her seat.

Dear Heavenly Father! she exclaimed to herself. *How does my fool of a husband propose to pay for all this?* Her face was still tear-stained, but there was new crying to explain it, so maybe no one would notice that she had come in that way.

Cameron was clinking a spoon against the side of his wine glass, which at this non-alcoholic affair was two-thirds filled with punch. He took a deep breath, determined to hold back (behind the mask of comedian-emcee) an increasing flood of emotions.

"A toast! To my beautiful and no-longer-so-blushing bride of these twenty years, Melanie Safka Henderson-hyphen-Lennox Gottlieb."

He nodded to his and Mel's tittering children, ages seven to eighteen, amused by the addition of middle and hyphenated maiden names that she would rather not acknowledge.

"Melanie Kafka, I mean Safka. Circumspect rebel daughter of respectable flower children. Beautiful people every one of them, but none more than she."

Mel shook her head and rolled her eyes. All these friends and relatives, her aging parents among them, were laughing along with him, whether or not they understood his allusions to Gregor Samsa's metamorphosis or that Sixties-era songster, her namesake.

"Oh, look what he's done to my youth, Ma, she's crying. Oh, bitter bad, heartsick sad, when you're over the hill forty years old and your old man won't shut his mouth and get down from the podium."

"Cameron. Shut. Up."

He winked at her. She tried to neither laugh nor cry.

"Yes, all of ye gathered here this evening for this birthday banquet, it's to Mel that we toast. This same foxy little lady who, slightly over twenty years ago, waved her pretty brown hair in my face, stealthily took my hand, led me off to her cultish church – in a trance, I assure you, in a trance! –"

"Please! Cameron!"

"– and said, looking Siren-like into my eyes: There's a chance love will come in my life, and baby it's you. So let's get hitched!"

Pretty Zoë Gottlieb with her high-pitched pink voice led the chorus of laughter at her cringing mother's expense.

"So, golly, that's just what we did. And here she is, five kids and not a headache later, we're as hitched as we ever were. And I'm glad of it."

"I bet you are, you old playboy!" Mongo shouted.

"Right on, man!" Mel's father echoed, standing on top of a chair at the back of the room.

"Condolences, honey," said a woman seated in front of him. "Does your sweetheart go on like that all the time when he prays over an ordinary evening's fixings?"

Cameron was clinking away again on the side of his punch glass. He struggled, against a growing wave of emotion, to keep the hint of a smile on his face, but his voice revealed a slight crack in that armor.

"Anyway, what I'm trying to get around to, is that I really do love her," he said. "And with that, all this joking stops. She's the love of my life, my justification for living. She's the beautifulest of the beautiful people, for honest-to-goodness real, my principal comfort in this crazy world. And anyone who doesn't understand why, just look at the gorgeous children she gave me."

He was about to ask someone to pray over the food being carted in when he thought he caught a wicked reflection from one of Zoë's facial rings and had an urge to tease her.

"Oh, except for that one, Bubble-Yum Top over there. She must be my fault."

*

Since he gave her that party last spring, not that she had really intended it, Mel didn't have the heart to leave Cameron. Instead, she started seeing a psychologist from Church Social Services, but he was a predictably straight-laced male and she felt uncomfortable making sensitive confidences to him. She traded him in for a woman about her age (Dr. Amanda Plotinsky) who was married to a popular local folk musician and singer – sometimes she was known to back him up on harmony – and who practiced an unpretentious brand of counseling that did not make Mel feel like a mental case.

In her weekly, then monthly counseling sessions, Mel talked about what was going on in her life and whatever else was on her mind. She talked quite often about the kids. Her oldest, Dylan, was serving a church mission in Japan and had written in a recent letter that he thought he would pursue his BA in Japanese language and comparative literature; he wanted to be both professor and poet. In her first session, she had spoken of her fear of all those North Korean missiles, of the complex of military calculations and misperceptions that might send them flying in his direction. She also spoke of Dylan's birth and the passion of young love that preceded his conception.

Before the fateful moment of love's first sight – when, in exchange for the pizza, she left Cameron the change out of her twenty and wrote her phone number on the back of his hand – Mel and her Mormon roommate had been listening to a taped copy of the soft-rock operetta *Saturday's Warrior*: crying together over the struggles of the boy-hero who, buffeted by the trials of this mortal testing, could not remember the promises he had made before his birth; dreaming of how they, too, would find the handsome boys who in that fabled, pre-mortal spirit existence they had promised to seek out and marry, of how they too would do anything (even descend to the very gates of Hell) to rescue them from temptation to the bliss of celestial glory.

Mel, at the time, was eighteen, a freshman with an undecided major. Cameron was a sophomore double-majoring in history and English. He was twenty-one. He had taken a year off between high school and college to visit his mom's Irish grandmother in Dublin, where he fell in love with hilly green landscapes and spent hours every day listening to traditional music and teaching himself, just for the pleasure of it, to play the fiddle.

She told Amanda everything: how he called her that morning at two-thirty, soon as he had gotten home from his shift; how she, who had been lying awake trying to remember all the sweet nothings he must have showered her with before they were born, picked it up in the middle of the second ring; how they whispered until the sun came up and then met at the student union for breakfast; how no more than a day later, on Sunday morning, he was attending church with her: he who had not attended a service of any kind since he'd been in Ireland.

A month longer and he would be baptized, just as she had been scarcely three months earlier after first attending services with the roomate who had invited her. And a week after his own baptism, Cameron was ordained to the Mormon version of a levitical priesthood so he could bless the holy sacrament. By the end of that school year, without either set of parents' blessing, they were engaged. The following autumn, given their urgent impulse to procreate and otherwise fashion a bit of heaven for each other, their bishop approved his ordination to the higher priesthood and authorized their recommends to attend the sacred temple where only the most faithful could attend, where they were married in a mirrored white room a week before Christmas of 1981. Cameron had emptied his savings in order to fly her out West. Mel's college roommate's parents in Bountiful, Utah, had let them spend the previous night, in separate bedrooms, at their house, then rose with them early for the trip to Salt Lake City, where they would guide their daughter's young friends through the unfolding mysteries of that sainted space.

Cameron had pre-paid for five nights at a mountain resort where they seldom emerged from their heated cabin, obtained for them by some miracle by the intervention of a friend of a friend of a friend, except for meals in the main lodge and an occasional romp in the snow. They never set foot on a ski or turned on the television. Sometimes, on a tape player they had brought along with them, they listened to Karen Carpenter or Al Green or the Osmonds, their religious theme album called *The Plan*, or to the soundtrack of Olivia Newton-John's *Xanadu*, that fluffy teen-age chick flick that she had dragged him to three times, or to his Irish favorites, the folkloric Chieftains. But these were merely background to their incessant talking, giggling, lovemaking.

Finally, back within their university congregation's

familiar embrace, they had sat glowingly for the first time as Brother and Sister Gottlieb. At home again they would lie naked under their covers where, after making love some more, they would take turns reciting Book of Mormon and Bible verses and the poetry of W. B. Yeats and Dylan Thomas, which in Ireland he had devoured along with the music.

Afterwards, still lying there, he picked up the fiddle he had left standing by the night table and plucked out the rough vestiges of a tune: first serenade ever witnessed (these giddy lovers, though vaguely hoping, could not know) by the bonny little baby boy they had just conceived.

*

Rosie, the second oldest child and first daughter, was studying on an academic and soccer scholarship and talked of serving a mission herself when she turned twenty-one; she resented the patriarchal chauvinism that restricted her from leaving at nineteen like her brother in case she should change her mind and get married, get started on her real task of rearing a family. Then Ruth, who had come along a year after Zoë (the third child) and whose Biblical name symbolized Mel's own decision, at a time of marital crisis, to stay with her husband wherever he might go, was in the regular high school's band and had placed First Division four years running at State Solo and Ensemble competitions for her performances on both flute and piccolo.

Mel cried telling Amanda Plotinsky of that spring and summer of '85 when she had been pregnant with and then delivered of Zoë. Cameron committed adultery one night, then brashly confessed it to Mel when he walked through their door. He had been tempted by another's belly, another pair of breasts, then repented with a zeal that left him tottering at an abyss. He had leapt in, then, and might finally have drowned in that abyss; or frozen in it, come winter, in the same Volkswagen that instead, these years later, he would escort her in to her surprise party.

He might have frozen to death there in that frigid Hell of his own making, within the cramped depths of that German marvel, but instead of further into Dante's icy flames, she yanked him back into life; it was now seventeen years since Mel jerked open the driver's side door of the car he had been sleeping in for almost three months and took Cameron back.

First, as his reclining shoulders and head slid out with their shifting support, she had screamed at him and repeatedly slapped his face and pounded on his chest. Then she cried. She stood back at the edge of that parking lot and looked up at the stars. She did not try to stop shaking or to wipe the tears streaming down her face. As soon as he caught himself there on the pavement and gravel, he went to her and held her. He was crying, too, and his back stung where he had scratched it. He was naked to the waist and barefoot. His jeans were cut-offs, half way on his thighs. She wore a jeans skirt to her knees and a loose T-shirt, un-tucked. Her hair was back in a ponytail. He wrapped his arms around her, below the breasts, and pressed the whole front of him against her back. She turned her face to her side, away from his five-day stubble that scratched her face. He whispered in her ear repeated sorries. He slipped a hand under her shirt and stroked her belly.

Already, awaiting whatever yawning fate the Mormon God and his unyielding prophets of family values might have in store for him, he had quit his doctoral program and gone to work the 4:00 A.M. shift at Otis Elevator and to mowing grass and cleaning the building of an area Unitarian-Universalist church, which out of an ecumenical sense of humanitarian concern and Christian charity took him in. They allowed him to wash up at the water faucet in the janitor's closet and to sleep in their building, if it suited him, but he preferred the personal Calgary of his car. A small fraction of what they paid him went to himself, and everything else he earned to the wife he had betrayed and the unwitting children.

But then she had taken him back. She led and he followed. At home, he picked the two heaviest children out of their seats where they had miraculously slept through that whole brawl. And Mel especially remembered this: his first gazing (wondrous, adoring!) at Zoë Elisabeth while she was cradled in her mother's arms; as well as first-born Dylan's sleepy awakening to his daddy's touch, the daddy he had feared might never come back. The checks, after all, having come to his mother in the mail, in security envelopes, with no return address.

After quieting the children back down and putting them to bed, Mel and Cameron stepped into and out of the shower and into their own bed where, dripping wet, they made love to each other, with mutual desire, for the first time since the first trimester of her pregnancy with this latest child, who had been born in his absence. In the morning, Cameron went back to church and faced that particular music. He was excommunicated and spent the next period of years gradually gaining his place back in that stern but welcoming spiritual community. First he was re-baptized and afterwards re-ordained to the higher priesthood. A few months later, he and Mel were re-sealed to each other in eternal marriage within the granite splendor of the Salt Lake temple where they were first married. Then the children were called from the nursery where they had been waiting on this detour from their Western vacationing. They were led to a white room with reflecting mirrors on every wall that made them think they were seeing the very eternal lives they were aspiring to. Cameron had been kneeling there at room's center at the white altar across from Mel; clasping his right hand with hers, their covenant hands, husband and wife smiling at each other, at each one's reflected image in the mirrors. Now they turned their gaze at each one of their four children (the fifth as yet un-conceived) as they were led in to their parents and knelt there, too, marveling at all those reflections that would bind them together: that day they had again become a forever family.

*

That fifth child was Dominic. He was an unexpected but pampered little rapscallion, cute as a button, who in a few months would be eligible for baptism and who his kindergarten and first-grade teachers whispered, among themselves, would be a perfect candidate for Ritalin.

Yet he was nothing next to what Zoë had become. Oh, Zoë! The question always had been, and still remained: whatever to do about Zoë?

"So what's she been up to this month, anyway?"

"Nothing new to speak of. Same old, same old."

Amanda Plotinsky had been seeing Zoë, too, since her parents had put their feet down and kept her home from a bikers' summer tour of the Atlantic and Gulf states, and caught her climbing out her window to join Mongo on his thunderously revving Harley. As soon as they let her out of the house after Mongo and his Marauders had gone, she took a baseball bat and was busy smashing in windows at an assisted-living facility when the police showed up. They flashed their siren once and called out to her to stop. She didn't even look back over her shoulder, just ambled along on her little spree. She put up no resistance when the female officer tackled and cuffed her and her male partner confiscated the bat. Now she was putting in her community service down there, making the rounds and visiting all those people whose windows she had broken.

Mel could hear rain falling outside Amanda's office. It was October. It might still get hot again, but now it was a cool sixty, maybe a bit colder.

"She's been going over there for three months, now," Mel said. "Says she likes one old cuss in particular, because every other sentence has a 'Gee-dee this' and 'Es-aitch that.' She just throws her 'Ef you, old codger' at him and gives a little twinkle with her eye. Both of which he returns at her and they go back to their game of chess."

"She tells me she enjoys her visits."

"It's a wonder her dad and I aren't being sued. We're lucky to get off with just that debt."

"Which you'll see she pays you back for."

"One can always hope."

"But, anyway, she's keeping out of trouble now?"

"If you consider running around with Mongo staying out of trouble."

"I think you shouldn't worry too much about Zoë. I think she still wants to go on to more school. Given enough time to finish all this acting out and assert her independence, I think someday she'll get it out of her system."

"Pray the Lord she lives that long."

"This forced volunteering is doing her some good, too. She tells me she might want to be a counselor. I think she could be a good one."

"She'll have enough life experience for the task, that's for sure."

The two women smiled and Mel shook her head. Amanda Plotinsky leaned back in her chair and raised a pencil with eraser to her chin.

"And Zoë's father? You mentioned him a moment ago. How's he dealing with all of this, right now?"

Mel turned her head to one side and closed her eyes. Her footwear, off-white nondescript tennis shoes, rested on the floor where she had kicked them off. She hugged her legs to her chest, chin against her knees, head tilted slightly to one side.

"I'll tell you. He was up in his attic the other night, I thought poring over some term papers. I stomped up those creaky stairs to tell him something, I can't remember what, and he didn't even hear me. He was on his knees praying. Beating himself up like after he'd cheated on me that time. He thinks it's all his fault. The state of his nation and world, the fact I can't figure out how to love him like I used to, and Zoë all hell-bent on her own destruction."

*

It was Monday, December 2, when the first rose arrived for Mel while she was bent over some detail work at an old-fashioned roll-top desk at the print shop. It was a small staff of three in an operation that would publish two or three titles in any given year. The owner and chief editor, Grace Tillman, widowed heiress to both her parents' and her husband's fortunes, enjoyed the luxury of producing pricey quality editions of only one hundred copies each. The first copy would remain in the adjoining reading room and the second be donated to the rare book collection at the Lilly Library in Bloomington. The production director, Jancie Jensen, was Mel's closest friend and a frequent visitor at the Gottliebs' outlying farmhouse. Mel was director of art and design.

The delivery boy, maybe Zoë's age and fresh from school, was standing in the doorway that separated their work space from the public reading room, presided over on an alternating basis by a trio of retired men and one woman who admired the enterprise and volunteered their time; whom Grace, nevertheless, richly rewarded at Christmastide and on their and family members' birthdays.

"This says it's for Melanie Henderson," the boy read. "I'm told there's a Melanie here?"

"Oh, my gracious!" Grace exclaimed. "Melanie Henderson. Who could Melanie Henderson's beau be?"

"Couldn't be her husband, that Gottlieb fellow," Jancie parried.

"Not Cameron Gottlieb. That romantic old fool?"

Grace was the first one there and snatched up the rose and the little folded card.

"'From a secret admirer,' it says. 'You color my world.'"

"That's a song title, girlfriend. Who was it? The Commodores?"

"Chicago."

"Oh, right. So who do you know listens to that old band, Mellie? Is it Cameron?"

"Well, it can't be, you already agreed. Must be some other beau. Aren't you paying attention, Jancie?"

"You're right. It couldn't be him."

"Not that romantic fool."

Seventy-year-old Grace, playing like a teenager while the delivery boy shrugged his shoulders and said good-by, held rose and card aloft, daring Mel to come after them.

"Give it here. You know darn well who it has to be from. I don't have any secret admirers anywhere in the world."

Jancie pulled Grace's arm down while Mel grabbed the rose.

"And I suppose he did listen to Chicago. He's got as many musical as intellectual tastes."

"Quite a romancer, that old fool."

Mel smiled at the rose, perfectly red and petals folded, almost ready to open out.

"Oh, Cameron."

She sighed and sat back down to her work. She set the rose on a shelf above her spread-out proofs, which showed a puzzled cat talking to a stubborn mule. As she sat staring at it, nursing the pit in her stomach that she still could not explain or dispense with, Jancie leaned into her and whispered in her ear.

"Don't be stubborn, Mellie. Don't be that ornery old mule. You know Cameron's a sweetheart and that he loves you."

*

The next delivery came that same week, on Friday the sixth. This time there were two roses. The others followed at one-week intervals. The third time there were three roses, the fourth time, four, and so on until February 14, that Day of Lovers when Mel and Jancie and Grace each puttered around the workshop wondering when the dozen would show up, and if this secret admirer would finally sprout a name.

They were always roses. And the roses invariably red, perfectly closed, waiting to open. They would always come to her workplace except over Christmas break when they were delivered to the house, where the whole family was generally home.

The first time, Cameron had seemed puzzled. Mel could not read for sure whether or not he was teasing her.

"A secret admirer, huh?"

He lifted it to his nose and took a sniff. He shrugged his shoulders, pursed his lips as he set it back in the vase.

"Melanie Henderson. How about that. Must be someone who knew you before we were married."

"Or who just hates *you*, Dad."

Zoë grabbed a piece of pecan pie, slathered it with whipped cream, and stuffed a portion of it into her mouth. "Making like you don't exist or something," she said, stuffing in the rest and rushing out the door, not bothering with a good-by or a sorry-to-miss-another-family-supper.

As the other roses came, five and six and up to eleven at a time, his reaction alternated between mild bemusement and a slow jealousy that she could not determine was real or feigned. Once he grabbed her around the waist, held her just as he had outside that Volkswagen almost eighteen years earlier when she had let him know she was going to keep him.

"You wouldn't really leave me, would you?"

"No. Don't suppose I would."

"I love you, Mel, don't you know it?"

"Yes, I know."

She turned her face to him and let him kiss her lips.

"I know you do, Cameron. I thank you for that."

Later, in bed, their bodies merged in a tender, methodical way. She still could not say the words; still did not know if she had enough faith in love or life itself to say them.

"Do you still love me?"

She rested her head against his shoulder and stroked his chest. Kissed it. "Why wouldn't I?" she finally said by way of an answer.

*

"I don't know if she does or not," Cameron said. He was standing in the school's parking lot on that blustery February morning, chatting with a colleague before going in. "I don't know what she'll say. My heart's in her hands, though, I know that. This is my chance to win her heart back, and I don't care what it's cost me. It's my last hope, I have to play it right. What do you think? Will she say yes, or am I a goner?"

Johnny Chapman, Cameron's ear that morning, just shook his head and clicked his tongue. He wore Mexican huaraches to Cameron's tan loafers; ponytail and goatee to Cameron's short-cropped hair and beardless face; jeans, Che Guevara T-shirt, and faded denim jacket to Cameron's brown slacks, button-down green shirt, and mismatched sweater.

"And the fiddle? You really sold it?"

"Going, going, gone."

As they walked up the path to the main entrance, he patted Cameron on the shoulder.

"Hang in there, man. You've still got all this," he said, gesturing at the building in drab disrepair and the students in all their multitudinous variety.

Then, in the two-hour Focus on American History and Literature class that the two of them team-taught, Cameron was struck from a new angle by Mark Twain's little-known gem, "The War Prayer," in which the acerbic satirist at his best (he feared to publish it during his lifetime) condemned the facile, self-righteous praying of God's elect on both sides of an unnamed conflict. What struck Cameron for hours afterward, even though he had read the words many times, was that now they might just as well apply (as to the present build-up to war in Iraq) to his own praying for love restored: perhaps by praying rain on his own crops, or victory on this field of love's battle, he was asking harm on someone else; maybe it was not in Mel's best interest for her heart to once more be his.

He wasted no time, anyway, in getting to the florist that afternoon. When he pulled up outside of the print shop, he checked himself in the rearview mirror and re-combed his hair. He entered, then, and dropping to one knee in front of her, pushed the roses into her hands. She sat down, mouth open in front of all those witnesses, her co-workers as well as the others peeking around the doorway from the reading room, while Cameron knelt there and proposed to her.

"Melanie Safka Henderson-Lennox, apple of my eyes and comfort of my nights, will you marry me again beneath an Irish moon?"

Within the batch of flowers were airplane tickets for two for the middle of June. There was a brochure for the Dublin inn where he had booked five evenings and then five more.

While she hesitated, crying, he fell back on Yeats:

Down by the salley gardens my love and I did meet;
She passed the salley gardens with little snow -white feet.
She bid me take love easy, as the leaves grow on the tree;
But I being young and foolish, with her would not agree.

"Please take me back into your heart," he whispered once he had finished his recitation. "I was young and foolish when we met, but the best thing I ever did was fall in love with you."

To all those protestations, to all the sighing and sniffling in the background, all Mel could think to do was throw down that bouquet and run to her car, sobbing.

"Oh, how could you ask me this in front of all these people? How could you ask when it's all I can do to get up most mornings?"

*

It was three months later. A week earlier, in solemn white, Cameron had baptized his youngest child, the irrepressible Dominic; now he wore somber black to give away Zoë at her and Mongo's biker wedding on the stone porch of a wide-mouthed limestone cave. Zoë was dressed in a psychedelic pink gown with a cluster of purple pansies in her hair. When her time came she said, in her high-pitched pink voice, "I sure as hell *will* marry you, my manly hunksome biker man!" When she heard her daughter say that, Mel suddenly felt eighteen years old herself. She could not keep from giggling.

It was only then that Mel realized she was starting to feel somewhat closer to her old self. And that Cameron would soon have his answer. Suddenly, she laughed again. She looked at her poor husband who, sure that he was losing both of those beautiful women at once, was hopelessly and soundlessly crying. Seeing him that way and remembering those words of Jancie's when the first rose had appeared – her voice like some animal trainer's from Circus City herding stubborn cats and burros and other alien creatures like Mellie herself, mournful mule that she had been for so long – the new bride's mom was surprised by a light flow of tears on her own cheeks and broke out once more in a laughter not quite distinguishable from stacatto sobs.

As the party moved inside of the cave for refreshments and other diversions, after Mongo's festive Marauders, in honor of the newlyweds, had set off a twenty-one gun salute and frightened every beast within a dozen miles, Mel took Cameron's hand and started him to dancing.

At Zoë's request, in an attempt to appeal to both the old-timers and the youngsters in attendance, the sound system that had already been set up outside – it was precariously attached by a plethora of extension cords reinforced with layers of duct tape to a portable generator, in the back of a covered pick-up atop a steep incline at the edge of the parking lot; the amplification, at cave level, aimed at an angle toward its gaping portal several yards away – this jerry-rigged sound system was belting out a screeching Seventies-era Led Zeppelin tune, which would be followed immediately by the pot-smoking Doobie Brothers: "Jesus is just all right, oh, yeah!" The smile did not leave Mel's face all afternoon.

Later, when Cameron pulled her to him and dipped her so far that he lost his balance on the cave's slippery floor, he fell with her and stained her silken blue dress; but, when by some feat of love's prowess (or Cupidian chance) he managed to land beneath instead of on top of her, it was just into his arms that she finally came tumbling; and, quickly gathering her wits, lifting her head to gaze half-mockingly down at him, Mel took his face between her hands and kissed him with her moist lips, moving on from his to face, eyes, ears, forehead, nose, even the senstive part of his neck that used to always make him moan. In the midst of so much amorous mayhem, like the college girl she had once been and sometimes wished (so often, lately!) to have back, she giggled in her lover's ear and, in the sweet magic of love's enchantment, with their children and all those guests looking on, with smiling Grace thinking *Not Cameron, that old romancer!* and Jancie's eyes flashing *What fools, these precious donkeys!* and Zoë reading in her hairy, lascivious groom's smirk *Go get a room!* –out of all this chaotic madness, out of love's own puckish lunacy, Mel whispered what she had already answered once in the days of bliss and ignorance, before fully tasting the monstrous, mystifying, life-nurturing fruits of carnal knowledge:

"Yes! I will marry you! Yes! Yes! Yes!"

Contributors

The Southern Indiana Writers' Group has been more-or-less together since 1992. We began meeting monthly in a conference room in a local hospital. We now meet weekly to exchange information and expertise on everything from computers to poetry. The group also serves as a critique forum (in the same sense that a pack of wolves serves as food critics). Membership is limited, but visitors are welcome and have been known to fit in so well they become members against their better judgment.

Bonnie Abraham After twenty-five plus years of writing letters disqualifying people from Unemployment Benefits, she retired in order to write something more pleasant. She writes stories (many with Biblical themes), poetry, and devotionals. Currently, she resides in Corydon with her mother's ghost.

Janet Wolanin Alexander Retired science teacher married to a biology professor, mother of 10 fur-children: 1 horse, 4 dogs, and 5 cats, custom horsehair jewelry maker, part-time dog kennel worker, writer of horse tales, trail rider.

Marian Allen lives in a big house in a little wood, which is not the only difference between her and Laura Ingalls Wilder. She has published stories in print and online magazines, including Marion Zimmer Bradley's *FANTASY Magazine*, *The Phone Book*, *PanGaia*, and *Oceans of the Mind*. She blogs at marianallen.com.

J. Baumgartle Jeannine writes poetry and fiction. She is a member of Southern Indiana Writers group, and a contributor to their many volumes of Indian Creek Anthology, and working on her fourteenth collection of an inspirational series for the Corydon Presbyterian Church. She loves to take notes as the spirit walks us through the seasons.

Brenda Drexler was a high school, middle school, GED, and college English teacher in a past life. After some major life changes and a root canal, she returned to school to become a psychotherapist. She is currently teaching at a local community college and proudly calling herself a writer. She is an avid reader of a variety of genres. The work she is most proud of includes three articles published in a local newspaper and an anonymous letter to a senior officer of an Army post (lets keep that little secret to ourselves). Her book of short stories, *Four Shorts for Your Bucket List*, can be found at Lulu.com and Amazon.com. She recently published her first novel, *Gracie and Marge: Kicking the Bucket Together*, with some absolutely zany characters that you will love at first sight. It can be found at CreateSpace and Amazon.com. Brenda is thankful for the feedback of her husband, sisters, and friends after they proofread her works in progress. She's indebted to the good people at SIW for their keen eyes in perusing the written word and their blunt honesty. (She plans to use that last sentence when she wins an Oscar or Emmy, or something.)

Ginny Fleming lives in what was once New Albany's northern-backwoods, though in the last half century, her "lil house in the tangled wood" has been incorporated into the fringes of the city's bustling northern retail district. She considers herself to be foremost a screenwriter, as it's her favorite medium. Applying finishing touches to comedy scripts and unending tweaks to half-realized novels insures she's always writing – whether awake or not. She has hopes of a republication of her suspenseful romance/mystery novel "Keys of Illusion" ("Scuba in the Keys with the proper Merman"). Filled with paranormal fantasy, Jimmy Buffett, "magic cats," scuba and a bunch of lavender stuff – "Keys" will have you wishing and hoping mermaids ... *mermen* are real.

Andrea Gilbey is the most southeastern member of the group – southeast England, that is.

She visits the group as often as she can to add some British colour (because that's how they spell it over there), whenever she can get leave from her day job as a footwear technologist. (Motto: breaking shoes so you don't have to.)

Andrea has published five illustrated children's books for pre-schoolers and upwards, and with SIW colleague Ginny Fleming, worked on the *Written in Our Hearts Cookbook* in aid of the Davy Jones Equine Memorial Foundation.

She is currently working on a sequel to her first novel, *Bottletops for Battleships*, which is set in wartime England.

Andrea lives in leafy Hertfordshire with her two cats.

T. Lee Harris is a scribbler of the lowest order. Not only does she pen lies about people who don't exist, but she draws pictures of them as well. Harris has also been known to aid and abet others by putting their scribblings into book form and even going so far as to devise covers for these publications. She claims she went to school to learn these things, but that shouldn't be held against anyone.

Harris is, in turn, aided and abetted by others in her assaults against literature. Among these accomplices are Per Bastet Publications, who have shamelessly published her untruths about an ancient Egyptian scribe and a magic temple cat and, also, her prevarications about a former football player and a 200-year-old vampire turned international law enforcement agents. Also implicated are Untreed Reads and Hydra Publications, who have promulgated her lies about a retired spy who keeps getting mixed up in other people's business, and the Southern Indiana Writers – possibly the worst offenders of all – who have repeatedly permitted her to commit her acts of literary vandalism with their Indian Creek Anthology Series.

Glenda Mills is a mother of four, grandmother of seven, who spends her days surrounded by approximately 150 children at the child care facility where she works. She lives with her youngest son, her sister, and her niece in New Albany, Indiana. When she isn't busy with work, family, church activities, or life in general, she writes whatever God places in her heart, or whatever project SIW decides to do next. She looks forward to the day when she has the time to take the many ideas in her mind and put them in print.

Brett Alan Sanders is a writer, translator, and retired teacher living in Tell City, Indiana. He earned a BA in Spanish (with an English minor) at Indiana University and an MALS (Master of Arts in Liberal Studies) at the University of Southern Indiana. He has been a contributing writer at *Tertulia Magazine*, where for "Tertullian's Blog" he wrote the occasional column "Arte Retórica," and a former columnist for the *Perry County News* (the best of those columns have just been published by Per Bastet Publications under the title *Confabulating With the Cows*). In addition he served a brief stint as managing editor at *New Works Review* and has translated for the literary-arts website *suelta*. He has published original essays, fiction, and literary translations in a variety of journals including *Hunger Mountain, Artful Dodge, The Antigonish Review, Confluence: The Journal of Graduate Liberal Studies*, and *Rosebud*. He has also published a YA novella (*A Bride Called Freedom*, Ediciones

Nuevo Espacio, 2003); two book-length translations from the work of Buenos Aires writer María Rosa Lojo (*Awaiting the Green Morning*, Host Publications, 2008 and *Passionate Nomads*, Aliform Publishing, 2011); and the translation of Argentine American poet Luis Alberto Ambroggio's poetic tribute to Walt Whitman (*We Are All Whitman*, Arte Público Press, 2016). He may be contacted via his website/blog at brettalansanders.wordpress.com.

Jen Selinsky was born in Pittsburgh, Pennsylvania. In 2003, she earned her bachelor's degree in English from Clarion University of Pennsylvania. In 2004, she earned her master's degree in library science from the same school. Jen has worked as a professional librarian for over twelve years. She has published more than 170 books, many of which contain poetry. Her work can be found on the following sites: Lulu, Amazon, Barnes & Noble, Kobo, iTunes, Smashwords, Pen It! Publications, and Books-a-Million, as well as many others. She has also been featured in publications such as *The Courier Journal*, *The News and Tribune*, *Explorer* Magazine, *Liphar* Magazine, and *Indiana Libraries*. Jen lives in Sellersburg, Indiana with her husband.

www.ingramcontent.com/pod-product-compliance
Lightning Source LLC
Chambersburg PA
CBHW070039260626
47159CB00005B/2086